I0619120

GRAVE MEASURES

THRESHOLD

KRIS NORRIS

NORRIS BOOKS

OTHER BOOKS BY KRIS NORRIS

SINGLES

CENTERFOLD

KEEPING FAITH

IRON WILL

MY SOUL TO KEEP

RICOCHET

ROPE'S END

SERIES

'TIL DEATH

1 - DEADLY VISION

2 - DEADLY OBSESSION

3 - DEADLY DECEPTION

BROTHERHOOD PROTECTORS ~ Elle James

1 - MIDNIGHT RANGER

2 – CARVED IN ICE

3 - GOING IN BLIND

COLLATERAL DAMAGE

1 - FORCE OF NATURE

GRAVE MEASURES

THRESHOLD

KRIS NORRIS

Grave Measures

Copyright © 2016, Kris Norris

Edited by Chris Allen-Riley and Jessica Bimberg

Cover Art by Kris Norris

Published by Kris Norris

Released ~ February, 2016

This is a work of fiction. All characters, places and events are from the author's imagination and should not be confused with fact. Any resemblance to persons, living or dead, events or places is purely coincidental.

All rights reserved. No part of this publication may be reproduced in any material form, whether by printing, photocopying, scanning or otherwise without the written permission of the author.

To my mom. Thanks for still having my back, even if you're watching it from the other side.

PROLOGUE

Come to me, Daniel. I'm waiting. I'll always be waiting.

"No!"

Daniel Cartwright bolted upright, his echoed voice still hanging in the room. Sweat stung his eyes as it dripped down his forehead, his heart pounding against his ribs. He tossed back the thin blanket and swung his feet to the side, the cool press of the hardwood floor grounding him slightly. He stared at his hands until his vision adjusted to the dark, not surprised at the tremor that seemed to have taken hold.

It'd been six months, and he still dreamt of her every night. Still felt the panic of having her disappear. The pain of finding her bloody. Broken. Dead.

Daniel.

He covered his ears with his hands, trying to block out the voice. *Her voice.* Not that it'd do any good. He couldn't extinguish what was already inside his head—what whispered over and over like a message on a loop. Drove him to the edge, only to disappear as the sun peeked above the horizon. But she'd return at the stroke of midnight. Test his sanity, once again.

An image flashed in his mind, the clarity of it stealing his ragged breath. She was dressed in white, her long chestnut hair lifting off her shoulders in the breeze. Those brilliant green eyes had filled with hope as she'd picked up her shoes and turned, walking barefoot along the path. She'd stopped and looked at him over her shoulder, laughing before daring him to catch her. Then, she'd taken off, the soft cadence of her footfalls slowly fading.

He'd waited. Given her a head start. Knowing he'd catch her before she'd reached the pond down the trail on the other side of the hill. He'd smiled, already imagining her silhouette flickering in and out of view amidst the trees as the path wove through a small copse—the source of their privacy once they reached the cool water. He'd pictured stripping her down—watching her pale skin gleam in the late afternoon sun. How she'd react to his every touch. How she'd feel moving beneath him, her body surrounding him, the slick slide of his cock mixing with the raspy sound of their breath. The way her fingers would clench his back as she climaxed around him.

After months of arguing and separate rooms, they'd decided to give their love one more chance. He'd taken her there—where they'd first made love. God, it seemed a lifetime ago. But he'd been willing to try—to give his heart to her one more time, even though a part of him worried she'd never truly be his. That his job would always stand between them—an invisible wall he'd never be able to break down.

His badge. That's what it was ultimately about. His shiny silver shield and the gun on his hip. Being a cop had been an attraction, at first. Full of thrill and intrigue. Then, the long shifts and lonely nights had started taking a toll. And she'd pulled away. Used every other excuse to wedge them apart, but he'd known the truth.

I'm waiting for you.

"Shut up, just shut the fuck up!"

He pushed to his feet, grabbing his pants off a nearby chair. He tripped toward the doorway, trying to tug the denim over his hips without stopping. It'd only fuel her power—give her more time to block his escape.

He stumbled into the hallway then headed for the foyer. The bedroom door slammed shut behind him as the lights flickered on then off, a low buzz filling the air. He didn't stop, barely registered the noise as he focused on the silver-colored knob thirty feet in front of him.

A chair scraped out from the kitchen table as he passed by, her ghostly silhouette wavering in and out of focus. He didn't acknowledge her—knowing he'd never get out if he looked at her. Saw the wounds carved into her skin. The bruised pattern around her neck. Of all the bodies he'd faced in the line of duty, none had been that devastating—that gutting—until he'd found her...

He shook away the thoughts. He couldn't have known. Couldn't have anticipated that bastard would be lurking. Waiting to steal her away. Take away his last hope at even the semblance of a normal life. That their game would end as yet another statistic. A number on a case file.

You knew what he was capable of. You never should have left me alone.

Daniel bowed his head as he palmed the doorknob, her words stinging as much, now, as when she'd first appeared to him. The air cooled along his neck, and he knew she was standing behind him—waiting for him to weaken. To turn around.

He twisted the handle, surprised when it actually turned. He'd lost count of the nights she'd trapped him there. How many times he'd been forced to relive that moment—see her death through her eyes. Shit, he didn't even know how she did it. If any of this was truly real.

Daniel.

He reefed open the door, staring out at the street. A light rain misted the air, blurring the glow of the lamplight into a wash of grays and yellows. He placed one foot beyond the threshold, willing himself out of the house, when icy fingers cupped his shoulder.

He froze, the sheer pressure of the invisible touch holding him captive. His stomach rolled in protest, the acidic taste of bile burning his throat.

He clenched his jaw, finally glancing back. The tattered remains of her short white dress hung off her shoulders—the red patches bright against the fabric. As if she were somehow still bleeding. Her once soft hair shot out in a tangled mess from her head like a fuzzy halo of dull brown. But it was her eyes that always took his breath away. Hollow and sad, with more than a hint of bitter resentment shining in the green depths. He'd never thought she could look at him like that. As if he'd been the one to steal her life away.

He blew out a shaky breath, noting the way it misted in front of his mouth. "Isabel."

She jerked back at her name, and he couldn't help but wonder if it held any power. If he affected her as she did him.

She recovered quickly, making the remaining chairs around the table shake. "You left me."

Her words bit at what little remained of his heart, her voice an eerie echo of what it'd once been. After months of hearing it inside his mind, it was almost a relief to have her speak aloud. A symbol of hope that she was more than a figment of his brewing insanity.

He shook his head, repeating the token saying that had kept him from giving in. From following her into the abyss. "Never. He took you from me."

"You knew how dangerous he was."

"Isabel, no—"

"You. Knew."

Daniel could only bow his head. He'd known Jacob had harbored feelings for her. But he'd never thought the man —his best fucking friend... He raised his gaze to meet her stare. "I'm sorry."

"Prove it. Come to me. I'm waiting for you."

"You know I can't."

"You can't? Or you won't?"

"Both, I suppose. Someone has to make sure he pays. It's my job—"

"Your job was to love me. Protect me. But you didn't love me, did you? It was over. You were going to leave me. Discard me like garbage."

Guilt soured his gut, heaving it in protest. "No. You know that's not true. I was trying to fix things. Fix *us*."

"Why didn't you follow sooner?" She seemed to hover closer to him, her feet not even touching the floor. "You wanted him to capture me. You wanted me gone."

She glared at him, this time breaking the glass next to the door. Pieces shot through the air, one cutting his jaw.

He didn't bother wiping at the blood. "No. Never."

"Then, come to me."

He set his jaw, firming his hold on the door as he finally turned away. "I can't."

He launched himself onto the porch, fighting against the pull of her icy grip. Scratches rose along his neck before he managed to break free—stumble down the three stairs to the walkway. Pain flared through his limbs, a sharp ache stabbing through his heart.

He twisted slightly, staring at the house, his gaze drifting to the glass. Solid once more, it reflected the eerie light of the lamppost, the flawless surface mocking him.

He closed his eyes. He couldn't live like this. Wondering from one day to the next if he was losing his mind. If anything was real, or if he was caught in some kind of endless loop. Groundhog Day from hell.

He drew a quick breath. He needed to stop the cycle. Break free of the guilt. Rid his mind of the memories. The nightmares. Find a way to move forward—do everything he could to put the bastard behind bars.

Bastard. Jacob. Daniel was going to ensure his best friend never hurt anyone else ever again.

The panicky sensation ebbed slightly, the feel of the cool mist calming him. He exhaled, spinning toward the street as he opened his eyes.

Isabel hovered an inch from his face, those dull eyes burning into black. "I'm done waiting."

Daniel gasped as his body flew backwards, skidding across the foyer and into the kitchen. The front door slammed shut behind him, the light in the hall flickering, again. The glass in the entryway frosted over, blocking out everything beyond the pane except the outline of a handprint as it slowly materialized amidst the white, smearing off to the right.

He scrambled to his feet, darting over to the cupboard as dishes rattled along the counter. A couple lifted up, wavering in the air before shooting across the room—shattering against the far wall. He did his best to block out the sounds—the scrape of her feet along the floor, the wheeze of her breath through her punctured chest—tossing spices and bottles over his shoulder until he found what he was looking for.

He spun, nearly dropping the box of salt as he watched her vanish, appearing several feet closer in the space of a heartbeat. Daniel tamped down the fear, opening the lid then pouring a steady line of white crystals around him—the lopsided circle flashing in and out of view as the lights cut out then popped back on. He had no idea if the token gesture would work. If what he'd witnessed on different television shows held any weight. Hell, a part of him believed he was still in his bed, imagining everything. But fuck if he had any other ideas on how to stop her. And just thinking about spending another night pinned to a wall—watching her die over and over...

Isabel screamed, racing toward him, before stopping at the edge of the circle, her body jerking backwards as it hit the salt. She hissed, trying to break through the barrier, again, only to recoil, bits of her flesh curling into smoke. Hard, bitter eyes gazed at him as she swept her arms up, sending all the remaining dishes crashing to the floor.

She bared her teeth—a glimpse of white amidst her graying silhouette. "I knew you didn't love me. You'll never be free, Daniel. I'll never let you go."

She vanished, the misty remains of her body slowly

fading. He drew in a few shaky breaths, trying to calm the staccato rhythm of his heart. In all the times she'd appeared to him, it had never been this bad. Never this violent.

He waited until the air began to warm, the icy glass thawing into streaks of dripping water, before gathering his courage. He glanced up the hallway. The light in his bedroom was on, again, a strip of yellow shining beneath the closed door. All he had to do was make it outside, only this time, he wouldn't stop. Wouldn't look back until the house was nothing but a reflected light in the ghostly fog.

Daniel placed one foot on the outside of the circle, waiting a few moments to see if she'd suddenly materialize. An eerie silence filled the house, nothing but his forceful exhalations registering in the stillness. He gauged the distance—fifteen feet. Maybe twenty. He only needed a few seconds...

He sprinted toward the door, feet pounding the floor as he reached for the knob, gasping when icy fingers wrapped around his ankle, tripping him onto one knee. He palmed the wood, still reaching for the handle as her nails dug into his flesh, burning lines along his leg.

He kicked at her hold, his foot passing through her torso as she tightened her grip, sending a stabbing pain up his body and into his chest. Black smudges smeared across his skin as a deep cold settled around his heart, the resulting pressure making it hard to breathe.

Isabel's face appeared in front of him, her smug smile glaring back at him. "Mine, Daniel. Forever."

He managed to slide forward slightly—wrap his fingers around the handle—when the damn thing turned in his hand. A man and a woman stormed through the opening, shotguns poised at their hips. The guy fired, a blast of white power bursting from the muzzle.

Isabel screeched, recoiling in seeming pain before winking out, the pressure in his chest easing. He fell onto one elbow, coughing as he tried to catch his breath, his vision dimming at the edges. A hand cupped his face, tilting it up. He forced himself to focus on the stunning blue eyes staring back at him.

The woman smiled—a splash of pink amidst the gray. "You okay?"

He furrowed his brow, trying to process the words when she snapped her fingers in front of his face.

"Detective Cartwright? I asked if you were okay?" She swept her gaze down his body, frowning. "Hey, Jimmy. Our friend's got lacerations on his ankle. More on his neck. Lots of burns and bruising, too." She brushed over the skin on Daniel's neck. "Fuck! Pretty damn sure he's got blotches of ectoplasm on him. That's a first. And I think he's in shock."

"Who the fuck are you?" He cursed inwardly at her amused smile, his voice more than strained.

She cocked her head to the side. "Okay, maybe not as shocky as I'd thought. The name's Arrynn. Agent Arrynn Baker. This is Agent James White, but we all just call him Jimmy."

Daniel glanced at the man in question.

The guy waved at him, giving him a wink. "Yo, Danny-boy. What's up?"

Daniel frowned. "Agent? For what organization?"

Arrynn handed him her badge. "An obscure department within Homeland Security. Look, I know this is probably a lot to take in, right now, but... Trust me. It's nothing compared to what you're about to discover."

He forced himself to swallow, nearly gagging in the process as he handed back her shield. "About to discover? You mean it's worse than..." He waved his hand at the interior. "This?"

"Oh, sweetie, this is nothing. You should see what vampires and werewolves do to a kitchen."

"Vampires?" He shook his head. "Fuck. I've gone mad. This is all a dream, and I'm probably in some kind of fucking facility, drooling all over myself while a bunch of male nurses feed me colored pills!"

Arrynn chuckled. "Actually, that's probably the most sane thing you'll say for a while. Too bad it's not true. What happened here..." She mimicked his wave. "All real. And it's just the beginning. But something tells me, you're up for the job."

"Job? What job? What the fuck are you talking about? How the hell did you even know to come here?"

"We've been watching you for a while. Seems your partner was...concerned. You've been acting a bit odd. A few of the things you said around him..." She shrugged. "Made him wonder if there was something else going on. Something paranormal."

"Paranormal? I thought you were part of Homeland Security?"

"There are all kinds of threats. We just investigate unusual ones."

"Fuck."

"Hey, be thankful. If he hadn't called it in, we never would have been watching from across the street." She whistled as she straightened. "Haven't witnessed a spirit toss a guy like that in a long ass time. And, when you didn't come back out…"

"This is crazy. It can't be real." He leaned against the door. "What do you want from me?"

"It's more what you want from us. I'm talking about a whole new reality for you, Daniel. One that starts with you taking my hand, and us getting the hell out of here."

She extended her arm, beckoning to him with her fingers. He swung his gaze to the kitchen, staring at the shards of glass and porcelain before releasing a slow breath. He looked up at her, clasping his hand around her forearm as she helped lever him to his feet.

An easy smile lifted her lips as she motioned to the open door. "Smart choice. After you."

He rolled his shoulders, limping the few steps it took to reach the porch. An echo of Isabel's voice sounded inside his head, the pleading words barely recognizable.

You're mine. Forever.

He took one more step, ignoring the mournful rasp of his name as he turned to Arrynn. "Where are we going?"

"Home. Your new home." She extended her hand, again, this time shaking his. "Welcome to Threshold."

CHAPTER ONE

"You know you only have to burn the bones, right? Not send the ashes into space."

Daniel clenched his jaw as Arrynn shuffled in behind him, her arm lightly brushing against his. He didn't turn, didn't make eye contact. He couldn't. Not without wanting to fucking scream. Grab her arms, give her a hard shake and demand answers he knew weren't hers to give. Make sense out of a reality that was so far beyond sensible, it wasn't even dust in his rearview.

He watched the flames lick at the bleached bones, the tiny sparks lifting into the air like hundreds of fireflies taking flight. "No harm in being sure."

She snorted. "Guess that's one way of looking at it."

He cursed under his breath, ignoring the warning bells still ringing in his head as he twisted to meet her gaze. "You got something you want to say?"

Arrynn shrugged, kicking at the sand with her boot. "I think you already know."

"Being thorough doesn't make me crazy." He laughed.

"What am I saying? We hunt fucking ghosts for a living. We're already crazy."

"We do what's needed so others don't have to know the truth."

He turned to face her, his hands fisted at his sides. "And what truth is that? That ghosts are real? Or that they'll fucking kill you if given the chance?"

Arrynn sighed. "Not all spirits become vengeful."

"No. But it only takes one to change your life." He spun, staring at the mix of orange and yellow as it rippled along the pile."

A hand cupped his shoulder, the easy weight nearly taking him to his knees. She moved in closer, her breath tickling the hairs on his nape. "You know it wasn't her fault, right? Dying the way she did..."

He pulled away from Arrynn's touch. He didn't want her pity. Her understanding. Fuck, he didn't want anything other than to bury every last memory. Find a way to get through the day without the overwhelming sense of guilt smothering him.

He shook his head. "I know it wasn't her fault. It was mine."

"Daniel—"

"This would all be a lot easier if everyone just stopped coddling me!" He glanced at her over his shoulder. "We both know it's true. I let her go off alone. Left her vulnerable. I was supposed to protect her."

Arrynn scoffed. "Oh, so now you're the one who murdered her? Only one man is to blame, and his ass is doing twenty-five to life, without the chance of parole." She closed half the distance. "All I'm trying to say is...at some point, you're going to have to forgive yourself. Move on. This..." She waved at the equipment spread out on the sand. The fire reaching toward the sky. "This is just a bandaid. A temporary fix. Until you deal with Isabel's death—"

"I've dealt with it."

"Oh, baby. You've done everything *but* deal with it. You hunt. You kill. You send a steady stream of spirits back across that veil, but you haven't come close to dealing with her death. I see it, Daniel. We all see it."

She glanced at the fire, then headed for the path, stopping behind him. "You know I care about you. And watching you fight her ghost at every turn—even when it's not there... It's not just killing you. We all feel it. I'm not saying you need to forget, just...let it go. Let *her* go."

He caught her arm as she moved past him. "It's not her I can't let go of. I know she's dead. I know that whatever we had... I'm not stuck in the past, Arrynn. This isn't a case of undying love or pinning for away for someone."

"Then, what?"

He let his head bow to his chest. "It's knowing I couldn't save her soul. That I let it continue until there was nothing left but anger. Blame. Resentment. That my legacy to her was letting her turn into the very monsters we hunt."

"You weren't a hunter, then. Hell, you thought you were imagining it."

"And now, you know why it haunts me."

He released Arrynn, shoving his hands in his pockets before he wrapped them around her and didn't let go. Until he'd sealed his mouth to hers to stop the screams.

Stripped her down and buried himself inside her until there was nothing left but them. This moment.

Arrynn sighed, the sound a mixture of sadness and resolution. "I'll be in the car with Jimmy. Make sure the fire's out."

Her feet padded across the sand, the soft scuffle slowly fading. Daniel stared out at the rising sun. He knew Arrynn was right. He needed to move on. Stop dwelling on facts he couldn't change. Find a way to make peace with the ghosts he'd never be able to banish.

I'm waiting for you Daniel. I'll always be waiting.

Isabel's voice echoed around him, the soft caress of her fingers along his neck making him jump. He turned, searching the beach, breath held, muscles clenched, only to stare into the unrelenting darkness.

Daniel hissed out his breath, picking up his bags before kicking sand over the flames. It must be the fatigue. His mind playing tricks on him. He'd seen to it Isabel couldn't hurt him, again. Couldn't hurt anyone. He'd won...hadn't he?

"Thanks for the lift, Arrynn. See you in a couple of days." Daniel shut the door to her car, taking a few steps away when the window rolled down. He glanced back over his shoulder, doing his best to keep his expression even— same way he had all shift.

Arrynn frowned, staring at the moon heading toward the distant horizon. "I didn't want to say anything with Jimmy around. Then, it never seemed like a good time..."

He arched a brow. "Say what?"

"You should have taken today off. Should have given yourself that luxury."

His teeth clenched together, and he knew the muscle in his temple was flexing with every damn breath. "I'm fine. Would have stayed home if I thought I couldn't handle it."

She snorted. "Fuck, you're stubborn. It's not about handling shit. It's about allowing yourself to be human, you dumb sod."

"Thanks. I think you're special, too."

He cursed as the words came out with more raw emotion than he'd planned. And fuck, he could tell by the way she inhaled, she'd noticed. Hell, she always noticed.

Arrynn sighed. "You've got my number if you decide you ever want to...talk."

She rolled up the window, checked over her shoulder then took off, her car quickly fading into the darkness. Daniel watched until the taillights disappeared before turning and walking up the path to his door. He climbed the short set of steps to his front door, drawing a deep breath before twisting his key in the lock and swinging the door open. A single light burned in the kitchen, the dull glow sending a shiver down his spine.

Didn't matter that he'd been coming through the door for months, he still expected to see some evidence of Isabel. That despite all he'd done—all Arrynn and Jimmy had helped him accomplish —he hadn't managed to fully free himself. That a part of her would always live on, even if it was just in his imagination.

He headed for the fridge, grabbing a Smithwicks before continuing into the living room. He kicked off his shoes, placed his feet on the coffee table and relaxed back, taking a long pull of the cold liquid. The beer soothed the edgy feeling prickling his skin, and he closed his eyes, allowing his mind to drift. He still couldn't believe he'd only been working at Threshold for about six months. God, it felt longer. Lifetimes.

An image of Isabel flashed in his head. One year. Today. Hell of a way to spend an anniversary. Shit, hell of an anniversary to have. He reran Arrynn's words. Burned his gut that she was right. He'd been off his game today. Distracted. He should have taken the damn shift off. Not put his partners' safety in jeopardy because he had something to prove. Because he couldn't admit that he hadn't wanted to be alone in the house all day. That he was scared the voice he'd been hearing was real.

Isabel's voice.

He pushed aside the thought. It was fatigue. Guilt. The fact he hadn't experienced anything other than random visions, words, was proof that it was all in his head. If she really was still around, surely she'd have made her presence known, by now. Broken dishes. Objects out of place. Flickering lights and cold shivers...

You'll never be free...

He snapped open his eyes, twisting his head toward the echoed sound. Nothing. He pushed to his feet, taking a few steps in that direction when the floor creaked behind him. He spun, his blood running cold as he stared at a faded image of Isabel standing beside the window— her head turned away as she stared out the glass pane, her white dress eerily bright.

He shook his head, standing his ground. "You're not real."

Her gaze swung to him, her eyes filled with sorrow. "Aren't I?"

"I did everything right. You're just my imagination."

She laughed, but it wasn't maniacal like it'd been before. "Then, you've got nothing to be afraid of."

"What do you want?"

"You know what I want, Daniel."

"I'm not going with you, Isabel. Figment or not...I know how to protect myself. How to fight back. You won't find the weak man you left before."

Her head tilted to the side. "I never thought you were weak. Quite the opposite. You were always too strong. Too dedicated. Out to save the world. Save everyone, except me."

He raked a hand through his hair, scratching at his scalp. "If I'd known... Fuck!" He grabbed the beer bottle and tossed it across the room, hitting the glass. Liquid splattered against the panes before the bottle crashed to the floor, breaking into a kaleidoscope of tiny shards.

Isabel flickered, winking out only to return. "When are you going to realize you can't ever get rid of me? That I'll always be a part of you. It doesn't matter how much salt you use, what you burn—I'll still be here. Waiting. I'll always be waiting."

He scrubbed a hand down his face. "No. This ends."

She frowned. "What's wrong? Don't you want me anymore?"

"You're dead. I can't..." He huffed out a breath. "What I want is for you to find peace. To cross over. To leave me the fuck alone to try and find some shred of happiness in this life. I need you to let go, this time."

Her image flared then dimmed. "I'm living in Hell. You should have to live in one, too."

She vanished, nothing but drops of beer shimmering on the glass.

"Fuck!"

He sucked in a few quick breaths, reaching for his phone. He unlocked the screen and hit the contact number before he had a chance to second guess himself. Arrynn picked up on the second ring.

"Daniel? Everything okay?"

He closed his eyes as he released his breath. "I...you want to have a drink? I could really use a drink."

A pause before her exhale sounded on the other line. "I'll pick you up in ten. Wait outside for me. And Daniel...I'm glad you called."

"Ten minutes."

He hung up, heading for the door. He didn't pause when Isabel appeared in front of him, continuing through her. A shiver of cold beaded his skin, but he ignored it. It wasn't real. None of it was real. He just needed to rest. He wasn't crazy.

CHAPTER TWO

Daniel.

Daniel jerked up his head, blinking the room into focus as he dragged himself back from the edge of sleep. Sunlight streamed through the windows, highlighting the specks of dust floating through the air. Another thirty minutes before the damn sun set and things really got interesting. The microwave beeped off to his left, the number pad flashing zero. Third damn time he'd reheated his coffee, and he had yet to remove it. He rubbed the back of his neck, tracing the scars that crisscrossed his skin, ignoring the way the marks seemed to burn from the simple contact. It was just fatigue getting the better of him.

You're mine.

His stomach tensed as the ghostly voice played in his head, again, the eerie sound openly mocking his sanity. Three years—today—and she still haunted him. Awake. Asleep. It didn't seem to matter. She merely waited until he'd managed to put himself back together before drifting into his life.

Forever.

He pushed her parting words out of his head, grabbing his mug. It was just his mind fucking with him. He'd vanquished her ghost. Burnt her damn remains and anything remotely connected with her. Done everything to send her spirit across the veil. Her presence was nothing more than a faded memory. An itch he couldn't quite scratch enough.

"Hey, Garret, look who it is?"

Daniel spun, clenching his jaw as two men entered the room. Garret Weston and Tanner Hastings. Partners who worked in the *were* division down the hall. They had more than a chip on their shoulders and had been riding Daniel's ass since he'd first arrived. Something about him being an ex-cop seemed to rub them the wrong way. Though, Daniel suspected it had more to do with them being massive douchebags than anything else. Fuck, he wasn't catching any breaks today.

Garret crossed his arms over his chest, giving Daniel a cocky grin. "Wow, Danno, you look like you haven't slept in a while. What's wrong? Casper giving you a hard time?"

Daniel bit back his usual retort at the nickname—just another dig against his previous life. He arched a brow. "Is it the full moon, again, already? Must be tough working three nights a month."

Garret's expression fell. "Doesn't work like that, asshole."

"Really? When's the last time either of you bagged a

wolf other than during a full moon?" He snorted as he pushed past them. "We all know you only hunt the newly turned. Seasoned werewolves are just too damn smart for you boys."

Tanner hooked Daniel's arm as he moved past him. "At least we don't waste our time chasing a fucking mist. Your unit's a joke."

Daniel yanked away his arm, drawing himself up, when boots clicked on the floor behind him. He turned as Arrynn entered, auburn hair bouncing behind her in a ponytail, amused smile tilting her lips.

She hitched out a hip, giving the men the once over. "Ah, what's wrong, Tanner? You boys get caught with your pants down, again? Feeling a bit inadequate, now?"

Tanner muttered under his breath, openly gawking at her. "At least we get to drop ours, honey. From what I've heard, yours haven't seen any action in years."

Daniel fisted Tanner's shirt, slamming him against the wall. "It'd be wise not to insult my partner."

Arrynn cupped his arm, giving him a tug. "Let it go, Daniel. He's not worth it."

Daniel huffed, bringing Tanner's face closer before shoving him away.

Tanner chuckled. "You ghost types are such a bunch of pussies."

Arrynn tightened her grip on Daniel's arm, half dragging him down the hall. She didn't speak, just headed for their office, her lips still curved into a smile.

Daniel rolled his shoulders, gently easing free of her grasp. "I don't know why you're smiling."

"Because, even after two and a half years, you still let

them get to you. They're assholes with more arrogance than sense. Boys playing dress up."

"Yeah, well, if they keep running their mouths off, someone's going to see they end up being wired shut."

Arrynn stepped in front of him, blocking his way as he tried to get through the door. "What's up with you tonight? I know these full moon nightshifts suck, but you're not normally this easy to goad."

Isabel's voice played in his head, again, a tattered reflection of her flickering to life behind Arrynn before vanishing. Daniel stared at the vacant spot for a few moments before exhaling.

He shook his head. "Nothing. I'm fine."

Arrynn glanced over her shoulder then back at him. "You don't seem fine. You don't normally get this touchy unless..." Her voice trailed off as she pulled out her phone, glancing at the face. "Shit." She tucked it away, her expression softening. "You should have taken today off."

He snorted, gently pushing past her as he walked though the doorway and headed for his desk near the far window. "I'm fine."

"No one expects you to forget. Grab your shit. Go home. Have a few beers."

He looked over at her as he placed the mug on his desk. "It's just another day like any other."

"It's the anniversary of her death. And, before you get all defensive, I'd like to remind you I saw her in action. Saw what she did to you—those scars on your neck. Your legs. How violent the attack was, and that was just once. I know it was going on long before we ever showed up on your doorstep. So, don't bullshit me and tell me you've dealt with all that when we both know you haven't." Arrynn invaded his personal space, her chest knocking against his. "You still seeing her?"

He clenched his jaw, ignoring the wavering image of white beyond Arrynn's shoulder. "You saw me salt and burn her remains. You know she's gone."

"Being gone and being out of your head are two different things. And those smudges under your eyes suggest you haven't been sleeping well. So, answer the question."

"I'm fine. Can we get to work, now? Damn phones are going to ring off the wall soon. And where the hell is Jimmy? Bastard was supposed to meet me last night. Jackass never showed."

Arrynn frowned. "We're not done discussing Isabel."

"Isabel's dead—"

"We're ghost hunters. We know that's only a change in venue."

Daniel sighed. "I'm over her. Over it."

"Never said you weren't. But that doesn't answer my question. Are you still seeing her?"

"Arrynn..." He palmed her shoulders, slowly easing her away. "I'm not going off the deep end. I'm just...tired."

She huffed, shaking off his touch as she moved the few steps back to her desk. "What do you mean Jimmy didn't show?"

Daniel sighed. This he could handle. Taking about Isabel... He scrubbed a hand down his face. Who was he kidding? It wasn't Isabel that unnerved him. Sure, cold day in Hell before he admitted she still appeared to him, but she wasn't what made his heart skip or his blood pound in his ears. That reason was leaning against her desk, arms crossed on her chest, her full, pink lips pursed into a delightful pout.

Two and a half years, they'd been sitting across from each other—partners, friends—and Arrynn still took his breath away with nothing more than a smile or a glance. He'd been slowly falling for her since she'd first cupped his jaw the night he'd left his old life behind. Joined the ranks of hunters employed at Threshold—started chasing the monsters that hid under the bed.

He half sat on his desk, giving her a guarded smile. "Not rocket science, Arrynn. I waited. He ditched me. Had to do the damn sweep by myself."

Her eyes widened then narrowed, a light flush coloring her cheeks. "You went ahead on the assignment alone?"

Daniel cursed inwardly. Fuck, he really did need to get some sleep. Wasn't like him to screw up this much. "It was nothing. Honestly. Didn't get so much as a spike from the EM detector. Whoever called it in doesn't have a clue what's paranormal and what's some teenage kids messing around in an abandoned house."

She lowered her hands, fisting them at her side—looking as if she wanted to toss something at his head. Or maybe wrap those beautiful fingers around his neck. "You know the code, Daniel. Fuck!" She blew out an audible breath. "Last time I checked, you had my number. Want to explain why you didn't call me?" She moved forward, once again knocking against his chest. "You got something you want to tell me? A reason you don't trust me to have your back?"

"Don't trust you?" He leaned in, making her palm his

chest in order to hold him back. "We've all been working our asses off, lately. I knew you'd been up for nearly forty hours straight. Thought you could use the sleep, especially with the full moon rising tonight."

He got impossibly closer, wishing he could close the scant distance and take her mouth with his. Kiss her the way he'd envisioned a thousand times over. "If giving a shit is not trusting you, then fine. Guilty as charged."

He moved decisively out of reach, stepping behind his desk as he rearranged papers and random objects on the top. Arrynn stared at him, mouth pinched tight, eyes wary. She raised her hand, looking as if she was going to touch her lips, before jerking away her fingers.

She firmed her stance, but her bravado didn't quite stem the tremor in her chin. "It was dangerous. I'd rather lose sleep than see you hurt. And you'd have my ass if I'd pulled a stunt like that."

His breath caught as heat swirled low in his gut. Damn, if she only knew how much he wanted her ass. And her lips, and her love... He drew a deep breath, hating the hint of womanly sweetness that teased his senses. Not perfume or some kind of spray. Just...Arrynn.

"I'll keep that in mind." He chuckled at her arched brow of defiance. "Fine. Next time, I'll call, and you can drag your tired ass to the scene."

She exhaled, but the flush didn't leave her cheeks. She kicked at the worn linoleum floor, looking as if she was going to comment further before nodding. She moved back to her desk, leaning against it, again. "It does raise the question...what the hell happened to Jimmy? Not like him to ditch a job."

Daniel shrugged. "Guy's been acting weird for a while now. Ever since he started seeing that new girl."

Arrynn frowned. "New girl? I didn't know he was dating someone."

"I heard him talking to her on the phone a few times. Shit about belonging to her. I don't know. Sounded one-sided to me, but then, who am I to judge? I just figured he'd spent the evening with her. Lost track of time. Though, I do plan on having a chat with him."

"Get in line. Jackass knows better than to put a fellow hunter's life at risk."

"Arrynn..."

"I trained him. He knows better." She finally slipped into her seat, shuffling through disks scattered across the top of her desk. "So...you didn't find anything? No evidence of a haunting, at all?"

Daniel settled into his chair. This was better. Talking about ghosts was safe—as long as she left Isabel out of it. He could rein in his thoughts if he focused on the job. Standing there, sparring with Arrynn...

He eased against the backrest, crossing his ankles as he rested his feet on the edge of the desk. "Nothing. No electro-magnetic spikes. No electronic voice recordings. Hell, not so much as a chill across my neck." He shook his head. "If I didn't know better..."

He sighed, allowing the words to just fade. He didn't need her thinking he was paranoid. That he hadn't left his years as a cop behind him. Hunters were different. They were decisive, acting quickly on whatever evidence was on hand. They didn't deal in conspiracy theories. Ghosts didn't behave that way, and the last thing he needed was Arrynn questioning his sanity. She already thought he was still chasing memories. He didn't need to fuel that fire.

Waiting.

The voice echoed through his head, mocking him, as a flicker of Isabel wavered by the doorway. He focused on a report he'd been filling out, telling himself it was the fatigue, when Arrynn appeared in front of his desk.

"If you didn't know better…what?"

He met her gaze, wishing his stomach didn't drop at the pure blue of her eyes. The easy tilt of her lips. He swallowed with effort. "Nothing."

"You suck at lying, Daniel. Always have. So, we either have this conversation, or we go back to the one where you're still seeing Isabel, because I know you were lying about that, too."

"I don't suck at lying."

"Fine, then I just read you well. Now, which road are we going down?"

He gritted his teeth. Damn, she got under his skin. He crossed his arms over his chest, meeting her expectant gaze. "If I didn't know better, I'd have thought I was set up. Sent there as a distraction or decoy. Something, because how often do we go into any location and not uncover a single shred of evidence? How many abandoned houses are truly void of any paranormal activity?"

The bridge of her nose crinkled as she considered his question. "I guess there's a chance, but… You're right. There's usually at least residual energy. A ghost murmur, or a death echo. But why would someone set you up like that? Then, not do anything?"

"You don't have to sound so damn disappointed that no one tried to attack me."

"I'm not disappointed. I'm confused. If you were sent there as a distraction, I'd have thought whoever's behind this would have seen to it you had some company... human company." She palmed his desk, leaning in.

His gaze strayed to the top swell of her breasts, the glimpse of creamy flesh kicking up his pulse. She wasn't large, her curves matching the rest of her lean frame—more tightly coiled power than feminine softness. But he liked that. Liked the way her muscles flexed beneath her skin. The way her long, auburn hair set off the different tones in her complexion. The way she owned a room simply by walking into it. The woman was stunning, and he was hopelessly lost.

"How'd you get the assignment?"

"The same way we get every one." He scoffed at her huff. "It popped up on my phone. No reason for me to question it."

"And he just didn't show?" Those creases over her nose deepened. "Did you try calling him?"

"Christ, Arrynn, are you trying to tell me you think I've lost it? Of course, I tried calling him. Multiple times. Even swung by his place, afterwards. No answer. No Chevy." Daniel lowered his feet, sitting forward, ignoring the way she seemed to occupy his entire field of vision. "Hey, I get it. A warm bed sounds better than traipsing around an abandoned house searching for vengeful spirits. Even Jimmy deserves a night. And nothing happened."

"This time. You got lucky, *this time.*"

He gave her a cocky grin. "Lucky's my middle name, sweetheart."

She snagged her bottom lip, looking ridiculously

adorable in a rare moment of indecision, before drawing herself up. "Regardless—"

"Baker. Cartwright."

Arrynn turned as Daniel focused over her shoulder. Tanner stood in the doorway, hands shoved into his pockets, mouth pinched tight. Garret moved in behind him, his expression equally grim.

Tanner nodded at them, his usual arrogance noticeably absent. "Call just came in from our contact at the precinct. He's on scene. Looks like a possible werewolf attack."

Daniel glanced at Arrynn, but she seemed equally confused. "All right."

Tanner scowled. "You two should probably tag along."

Daniel snorted. "Tag along? With you?"

"Just...grab your shit, and get in a car. We'll meet you there."

"And where, exactly, are we meeting?"

Tanner sighed, glancing at his partner before raking a hand through his hair. "Seven twenty-five Orchard."

Daniel's stomach dropped, the inklings of fear crawling down his spine. He pushed to his feet, grabbing his jacket off the back of his chair. "Are you sure that's the right address?"

"I wish we weren't, I really do. But we checked it twice."

Daniel nodded, rounding his desk then offering his hand to Arrynn. "I'll drive."

She walked woodenly to her desk, retrieving her jacket before glancing back at him. "I don't need you to coddle me. I recruited you, remember? And I'll drive. Last thing we need is you skidding off the road because you're exhausted."

He hooked her arm before she could follow after the men. "Arrynn. This isn't some random call."

"You think I don't know that?"

He softened his voice. "If it's Jimmy—"

"You said he wasn't home. No truck!" She pursed her lips, rolling her shoulders back as she visibly calmed herself. "I'll be fine, just...I'm driving."

CHAPTER THREE

Arrynn Baker focused on the road, going through the motions as she shifted gears and changed lanes, following Tanner's black SUV as it headed across town. The moon glinted low on the horizon, brightening the clouds with a punch of yellow light. She didn't look at Daniel sitting next to her. Couldn't. Not without seeing the guilt reflected in his eyes. Hell, he'd been at Jimmy's house yesterday. If it turned out the man had been there, alive but injured...

She swallowed the ball of fear that threatened to claw out of her throat, doing her best to detach herself. Continue on autopilot. Regardless of what they faced, she had a job to do—*they* had a job to do. And getting emotional wouldn't solve anything.

She sighed at the thought. Hell, she'd been emotionally detaching herself for over two years. Ever since Daniel had grasped her hand and taken the first step toward his new life—a life she wouldn't wish on anyone. But someone had to face the terrors most people thought were myths. Fabricated stories. And Daniel had turned out to be one hell of a hunter. Quick. Determined. Calm. Guy didn't seem to let anything get to him—not since he'd walked out of that house and left Isabel's ghost behind.

She frowned. She knew he'd been lying about not seeing Isabel, the slight shift in his blue eyes, the hint of a flush on his cheeks both indicators. And the fact worried Arrynn. He was right. She'd witnessed him salt and burn Isabel's remains and anything he thought could give her a tangible link to this side of the veil. Hell, he'd made the pyre so big Arrynn had sworn he was trying to signal the damn space station. And yet, she knew Isabel's ghost still haunted him. Arrynn just wasn't sure if it was real or in his mind. If the guilt he'd ignored—shoved aside—was slowly picking away at his sanity. If this was the first sign he was on the edge of a very ugly breakdown.

She pushed aside the thoughts, focusing on the job at hand, which, fuck, wasn't any better. But worrying about Daniel made her edgy—as if her skin didn't quite fit right. All he had to do was flash her that boyish smile and her stomach did somersaults. Even now, she had to resist reaching for his hand—finding strength and comfort in his touch, however innocent. Knowing that she could face anything as long as he was there, at her side. Though, she didn't want to stop there. She wanted Daniel in every way imaginable. Hers. Forever.

She cursed the thought as it formed. God, she sounded as bad as some of the spirits they hunted. Possessive. Desperate. And she hated to admit the drive was killing her. Wondering what they'd find. If they'd somehow failed Jimmy. She slowed her car to a stop as she pulled up to the curb outside of his house. Flashing lights filled the night, a piece of yellow tape already strung across the doorway.

Arrynn took a deep breath, mentally psyching herself up as she grabbed the handle, shoving open the door. She swung one leg out, halting when Daniel grasped her forearm. She cocked her head slightly but didn't look at him. "They're waiting."

Daniel huffed, his grip still firm. "And they can wait one more minute."

She sighed. "Whatever's inside that house, sitting out here agonizing over it won't change the outcome."

"Pretending it's not going to gut us isn't much better. Trust me. I have a bit of experience finding someone you care about butchered. You're never truly prepared for how it's going to feel. Or how it'll affect you. Just..." He cursed, reefing open his door. "I'm really starting to hate this particular date."

Arrynn cringed. Fuck. In the short amount of time it had taken to drive across town, she'd forgotten that it was the anniversary of Isabel's death. The day that had changed Daniel's life forever. Facing another loss on that same day...

She stepped out, joining Tanner and Garret before continuing to the porch. A man in jeans and a button-up shirt greeted them, shaking Tanner's hand.

"Not exactly how I wanted to see you, again, Tanner."

Tanner merely nodded, glancing at her and Daniel. "This is Detective Barry Stevens. He, along with Daniel's old partner, Ryan, keeps us informed if any cases look paranormal in nature. Mostly *were* or vampire attacks. Acts as a liaison with the various precincts throughout the city.

Helps keep the questions regarding our department to a minimum We appreciate the call."

"When I saw the ID badge, then the way he was killed, I knew you'd want in on it." Barry winced. "I'll admit. It's pretty ugly."

"How much time do we have?"

"About twenty minutes. When I explained to the other officers you're part of Homeland Security, and the victim was one of your own, they agreed to let you have a quick look around. Just don't touch anything, okay? They aren't quite sure why DHS would do their own investigation into an apparent animal attack, and they don't really seem like fans of *X-files*, if you get my drift."

Tanner raised one hand. "Scout's honor." He glanced at her and Daniel. "You two ready?"

Daniel clenched his jaw then struck off, ducking under the tape as he followed the other men inside. Arrynn took a deep breath, drawing herself up as she stared at the open door. Fuck, how many times had she walked through that entryway? Arms loaded with beer, a movie tucked under her chin. Listened while Jimmy bragged about his newest conquest, knowing full well the man only got lucky about a quarter of the times he'd claimed. Of all the things she'd considered…

That damn ball welled up in her throat again, but she forced it down, covering the last bit of distance. The house seemed strangely quiet as she scanned the foyer for any signs of a struggle—frowning when nothing appeared to be out of place. Photos still balanced on a few tables, a half empty beer can leaning against one of the frames. A couple of work bags had been shoved next to the closet, Jimmy's badge tossed on top. His coat had been slung over a bench seat, his truck's key hanging on a hook beneath a mirror. She fingered the metal as she walked past it, wondering where the hell his truck was, before coming to an abrupt halt. A smeared trail of blood stained the floor several feet in front of her, the path leading through the next doorway and around the corner.

Tanner and Garret stopped beside her. Tanner gave her shoulder a light pat before they continued toward the kitchen. Arrynn bit back the sob tight in her chest, slowly walking toward the room. Her pulse pounded inside her head, the frantic beat making it hard to breathe. One of the uniformed officers gave her a sympathetic nod as she paused just shy of entering, mentally preparing herself for what she envisioned awaited her, only to gasp when she finally caught sight of the body, the bloody remains heaped on the floor. She stared at the corpse—her friend—wondering what the incessant mumbling noise was, when Daniel gave her a hard shake.

"Arrynn!"

She sucked in a shaky breath, finally dragging her gaze from the exposed bone to Daniel's face. Pain and guilt warred in his eyes, tempered by what she thought was concern.

He stepped in front of her, blocking her view. "Go get some air."

She shook off his hold, taking a step back. "Fuck that. I've seen more ripped up bodies than you."

"That so? How many were family to you?"

She'd never really had a family, and he knew it. "That doesn't matter—"

"Bullshit! I don't care how many scenes you've been to —it's different when it's one of your own. And Jimmy wasn't just a colleague. To either of us." He cupped her shoulder this time. "I know the onset of shock when I see it."

She clenched her jaw, holding it firm until the muscle started to ache before breaking eye contact. "I was startled. I'll grant you that." She looked back at him. "But I'm fine, now." She cocked her head to the side at his pointed look. "Swear."

He sighed, shaking his head. "You are stubborn." He released her, spinning around. "Body's cold. Blood's dried. He's been dead a while."

She nodded, stealing her resolve as she moved out from behind him, edging closer to the body. "Probably why he didn't meet you. He'd already been attacked."

Daniel glanced at her, mouth pursed before he sighed again. "Just thinking he might have been in here, dying, while I was on that fucking stoop, knocking, cursing his ass—"

"Daniel. Look at his wounds. You know as well as I do that he bled out in a matter of minutes. Other than maybe bagging the bastard that did this, you wouldn't have changed the outcome." She raked her fingers through her hair, ignoring the way her hand trembled. "Christ. Haven't seen something this graphic in a long time, if ever."

Daniel crouched next to the body. "Maybe Tanner's right. Maybe we aren't quite as tough as the other divisions."

"That's bullshit, and you know it." She shook her head. "None of this makes any sense. No way Jimmy got attacked without putting up a fight."

"Look around. There aren't any signs of a struggle. Not

so much as a damn cushion out of place. Not a chip of broken glass."

Arrynn glanced at the cop, ensuring he was out of earshot before continuing. "Then, the werewolf shifted back and straightened things."

"A werewolf with a neat fetish?"

Arrynn inched closer. "I've been hunting with Jimmy for over five years. He wouldn't have been an easy target."

"I'm not saying he would have been—it's just..." Daniel nodded, glancing around the room. "What if it wasn't a *were*?"

Arrynn coughed as she swallowed, the stench of the body starting to fill the room. "He's been torn apart."

"Other creatures can do that. A vampire."

"Too much blood. They'd never waste it like that."

"Changeling?"

"There'd be evidence that they'd shed their skin somewhere in here. It happens moments after they feed. And that shit doesn't really clean up." She sighed. "It looks like a wolf attack."

"You honestly believe he let a stranger in his house. That he didn't pick up on the fact the guy was a werewolf...then didn't so much as toss something at the bastard when he shifted?"

"Maybe our *were's* female."

"Maybe. Explains how it got inside, but... Shit, Arrynn. If it weren't for him being shredded, I'd swear this was anything *but* a werewolf attack."

She crossed over to him, lightly touching his arm. "What's your gut telling you?"

His eyes narrowed. "You'll think I'm crazy."

She gave him a nudge. "Already think that, so..."

Daniel exhaled, shoving his hands in his pockets. "Vengeful or violent spirit. Poltergeist. Spector, maybe."

"You think a ghost did..." She waved at what was left of the body. "All of this? Killed Jimmy like that?"

"Explains how he was taken by surprise. Why he didn't fight back. Nothing to fight against." He blew out a slow breath when she merely stared at him. "Look. I know you're the ghost expert, but... All that shit Isabel did to me. Shattering objects, glass. Cutting me with it then having it all become whole, again. Kicking and punching, only to have every countermeasure go right through her. Holding me prisoner inside that damn house, then I'd wake up back in my bed—questioning if it was even real. The scars she gave me. Call it a hunch if you want, but this—the way the air's charged, the lack of any physical evidence—*this* is how it felt in that fucking house every night until you gave me the strength to leave."

Arrynn's eyes burned at his words, the bitter honesty stealing her breath. He'd rarely mentioned that day in the past two and a half years. Had often acted as if it was a story instead of a memory. And she knew he hadn't spoken the words lightly. That it'd crushed a bit of his soul to admit it.

She nodded, praying her voice didn't crack. "Let's assume, for a moment, you're right. This kind of violence doesn't just crop up suddenly. How the hell did Jimmy not realize he had a vengeful spirit living in his house? He was a ghost hunter, for fuck's sake."

"I know. It all sounds so damn crazy."

"Admitting you have a problem is half the battle, Danno."

They turned as Tanner's voice carried across the room.

He and Garret walked over to them, occasionally glancing back at the cop still standing watch at the door.

Tanner arched a brow. "So, other than the obvious, what's crazy?"

Daniel's mouth pinched tight, and he seemed as if he wasn't quite sure if he wanted to share his idea before he exhaled a rough breath. "This. I know what it looks like, but it's not a werewolf attack. A ghost killed Jimmy."

Garret scoffed. "You're trying to tell us a ghost..." He pointed at Jimmy. "Did that? Shredded him down to the bone? No fucking way. Ghosts are..."

"What? Weak? Passive? Friendly like Casper?"

"Don't patronize me, Cartwright. I know they can be dangerous." He gazed at Tanner "Fuck. Never thought they could kill you. Not like that."

Daniel took a few steps closer. "Tell me, Garret. Still think we're pussies?"

Garret cursed under his breath as Daniel turned, kneeling beside the body, again. "Not that we're convinced you're right, but we checked the house, the perimeter. Nothing. Not a single tuft of fur or footprint. And the place is so damn neat. Never been to an attack where the inside didn't look as if a bomb had gone off." He moved in beside Daniel, nudging the man's shoulder. "Not to be a buzzkill, but some proof would be nice."

Daniel glanced at the cop, ensuring the man was still staring down the hallway, then pointed at a black smudge on Jimmy's pants. "I could be wrong, but I'm pretty fucking sure that's ectoplasm."

Arrynn leaned in. "Well, shit."

"Tanner."

They glanced at the doorway as Barry's voice filled the room.

The man tapped his wrist. "Just got word that the CSI guys are five minutes out. Might be best if you weren't here when they arrive."

Daniel stood. "Can we take a few pictures? Get some samples?"

Barry sighed. "I promise I'll have the techs swab and photograph everything. I've got a pretty good idea of what to look for. And I'll see that the evidence is returned to your center once we're done."

"How long will that take?"

"Four or five days. A week, tops." Barry held up his hand at Daniel's huff. "I know. Believe me. I'd be pissed if I were in your shoes. But..." He scrubbed his hand across his jaw. "Unless you want to answer a whole lot of questions about what it is your department investigates, we need to let it play out. I give you my word you'll get everything. His clothes, his cell. And I'll have them take pictures of the entire house, inside and out."

Tanner gave Daniel a pat on the back, heading for the hallway. "Man's got a point. Thanks, Barry. We'll see ourselves out."

Arrynn swatted Tanner in the shoulder once they'd made their way back to the man's SUV. "We could've called the director. Gotten jurisdiction."

"Not without an interagency incident."

"I don't give a shit about bureaucratic dick measuring."

"Neither do we, but we need to be smart about this. And the last thing we need is have half of Seattle's police department wolf hunting every full moon." Tanner raked his hand through his hair. "I get we don't always see eye-to-eye, but we're on your side. Jimmy was family. We'll get whatever did this to him. Besides, the extra time will give us a chance to launch our own investigation. Trace his movements over the past few weeks. Dig up more information. Then, once the coroner rules this a wild dog attack or some equally lame-ass story, we'll get all his stuff delivered to us."

Daniel scoffed. "So, we just go back to work and pretend as if this never happened?"

"Hell, no. You two are going to go back to the center, get your shit, and go home. Get drunk. Fuck. Whatever gets your mind off of this. You can look at it fresh tomorrow. When you're not clouded with guilt and anger."

Daniel gawked at him. "We're more than capable of doing our job, despite the circumstances."

"Never said you weren't. But you two would tell us the same thing if it were one of our team. Just trying to do the right thing, here."

Daniel muttered something Arrynn couldn't make out then headed for her car. She thanked the other men before sliding into her vehicle. Daniel didn't say a word as she pulled into the street. The heavy silence between them made it hard to breathe as she returned to the center, parking in the back next to his Renegade.

She shut off the car, finally looking over at him. "Go home. I'll have dispatch page us if anything important comes up."

His hands fisted in his lap before he yanked open the door and stepped out, slamming it behind him. She followed, rounding her car and marching over to him as he leaned against his vehicle, body vibrating with barely restrained anger.

She gave him a light punch in the shoulder. "Hey, I'm not happy about this, either. But Tanner was right. We don't have our heads on remotely straight, right now, and it's not some pissed off kid we might face. Going hunting like this…" She raked her hand through her hair, not caring if it she pulled most of it out of her damn ponytail. When he didn't make eye contact, she huffed.

"Damn it, Daniel! You don't have the monopoly on guilt, here. I haven't been over to Jimmy's place in a month. Hadn't been paying enough attention to realize he'd started seeing someone. That maybe there was fucked-up shit going on at his damn house he didn't want to tell us about because he thought he was hallucinating or could take care of it, himself. Christ, that he shouldn't bother us with it because god forbid we might think he wasn't good enough to stay on the team."

His breath made tiny clouds in front of his face as his gaze finally fell to hers. "I don't want you to make me feel better, Arrynn."

"Then, what in the hell do you want?"

The muscle in his temple jumped a moment before he grabbed her arms, pivoting until her back pressed against his car, her body trapped by his. One of his hands palmed the door beside her head, the other clenching her hip. His chest heaved as he closed the scant distance, his mouth brushing across hers then lingering an inch away. "To forget."

CHAPTER FOUR

Don't fucking do it, Cartwright. Can't uncross that bridge.

Daniel flipped off the voice in his head—the one that had kept him away from Arrynn this long—as he slanted his lips over hers, humming at the smooth glide of her mouth against his. She inhaled, granting him access, as he swept his tongue along her lower lip, teasing the soft flesh before dipping inside. Sweet essence with a hint of coffee filled his senses, the firm tangle of her tongue against his making him moan.

He moved his hand off the metal frame, sliding his fingers through her hair, using his hold to tilt her head back—deepen the kiss. Her hands landed on his shoulders, her palms skimming over his collarbones to lock at his neck, lightly scraping his skin. Her nails sent shivers skittering along his spine, making his dick harden painfully against his zipper. Shit, one touch, and he was ready to come in his pants like a fucking teenager.

He drew on some inner source of control, managing not to rip off her shirt as he released her mouth, kissing his way down her neck and across the upper swell of her chest, teasing her nipple through the thin fabric. It pebbled against her bra as a harsh moan escaped her lips.

"Daniel...god..."

The breathy quality of her voice only spiked his need, her desire clear in the way she tilted her groin against him, notching the hard ridge of his cock against her cleft. She hummed her approval as he stepped into her, flattening her against his Jeep, again, keeping her molded against him as he nipped and sucked at her nipple, wondering how long he'd have to release her to yank her damn top out of the way.

Arrynn tugged on his hair, another moan sounding between them as he slipped his hand under her shirt, skimming it up her ribs before pulling the neckline down —exposing her bra. He ignored the slight sting of her grasp, trying to work his way behind the clingy fabric when twin beams broke the darkness as a vehicle turned into the private lot.

Daniel jerked up, chest heaving as he attempted to focus over the top of his Jeep. A red truck slowed to a halt at the other end of the open space, a tall, heavily muscled guy stepping out. Styx—one of the vampire hunters— though Daniel didn't know the man all that well, other than that he was coolly detached and one hell of a slayer. He barely gave them a glance before grabbing a bag out of the backseat and heading inside.

Arrynn touched Daniel's jaw, regaining his attention. "Trust me. Styx doesn't give a shit."

Daniel moaned when she claimed his mouth, her kiss as desperate as his had been. He palmed her back, holding her tight, loving the way she hummed against his lips as her fingers flexed and released in his hair. He smiled against her neck, inhaling the mixture of autumn rain and woman—wondering if he could last the thirty-minute drive to his place, or if he'd simply take her there in the damn parking lot.

Images of the blood-smeared floor from Jimmy's house lingered in his mind. It could have been Arrynn. Her blood. Her body. Her soul he'd lost. All without ever telling her how he felt. Hell, that he was capable of feeling anything other than good-natured friendship.

You'll never be free…

He stopped, the warm feeling in his chest quickly turning to ice as invisible fingers scratched a line across his nape. He tried to steady his breathing, reminding himself it was all in his mind—that he'd vanquished Isabel's ghost.

Mine…

Her voice sounded next to him, and he twisted, watching her flicker amidst the darkness, nothing more than an echo of substance hanging in the air before completely vanishing.

"Daniel? You okay?"

Numbing cold settled in his gut. He clenched his jaw, slowly moving back as Arrynn dropped her hands to her sides. Lines furrowed her brow, but she didn't say anything as she glanced behind him, stepping away from his vehicle.

He attempted a smile, knowing he'd failed. "You were right. We should head home. Find a way to make sense of…" He blew out a raspy breath. "I…I'll see you tomorrow." He reached for the door, stopping when she placed her hand over his.

"There something you need to tell me? Because I know for a fact this has nothing to do with Styx or Jimmy." She eased her hand away but held his gaze. "Daniel."

"Nothing. I shouldn't have…" He waved at the space between them.

"Pretty damn sure I was on board…"

He huffed. "We just spent the past thirty minutes trying to decipher how our friend got shredded. Trust me. Neither of us are thinking clearly."

Hurt flashed in the blue depths as she crossed her arms over her chest. "So, kissing me…*touching* me… That was just a big misunderstanding? Is that what you're trying to tell me?"

He didn't miss the waver in her voice, or the red slashes across her cheek bones. "I didn't mean…" He blew out another breath. "I'm just trying to avoid being a mistake you regret."

"Sounds like you're the one who's afraid of regretting something."

She'll die, just like I did. She's not safe around you, Daniel. No one's safe around you.

Daniel clenched his jaw until it started to cramp, resisting the urge to cover his ears—block out the lilting echo of Isabel laughing. Now wasn't the time to lose it.

Gentle hands cupped his face, and he opened his eyes, staring down at Arrynn.

She brushed her thumbs along his cheeks. "Talk to me."

He placed his fingers over hers, gently easing them free. "Nothing to say. I'm fine, just tired."

"You're starting to scare me."

He gave her hands a pat, choosing not to comment

further. "Call me if anything pops up. Otherwise, I'll see you back here, tomorrow night."

He opened the door, sliding in and starting the car before he could change his mind—take Arrynn in his arms and refuse to let go. Isabel's voice echoed inside the confined space, and he revved the engine, determined to drown it out. He didn't look at Arrynn, backing up and heading out without so much as a sideways glance. The cold feeling inside the vehicle gradually dissipated, leaving him alone with his thoughts—visions of Jimmy playing in his head. There was something familiar about the wounds...the hint of a pattern amidst the carnage.

He scrubbed a hand down his face as he pulled into his driveway, parking beside the small building. Living on the outskirts of town, bordering a lake, definitely added some time to his commute, but damn, it never ceased to offer him a sense of peace.

Peace. What a joke. And not something he'd find anytime soon.

He walked up the short path, unlocking his front door before swinging it open. A single light burned in the kitchen, the soft glow easing a bit of the tension straining his shoulders. He kicked the door closed behind him, not bothering to lock it, well aware that humans were the least of his concerns. And locks didn't stop ghosts.

He tossed his keys on the small side table, setting his bag down beside it, then ambled over to the fridge. He grabbed a beer, popping off the cap before taking a long pull. The cold liquid soothed the heat still curling beneath his skin, the remembered feel of Arrynn's body pressed against his far too fresh to vanquish completely.

God, she'd felt better than he'd imagined. Firm

muscles flexing beneath smooth, soft skin with just enough curves to dispel any doubt she was all woman. The lingering image of her nipple beaded against her bra teased his senses, and he wished he'd ignored the damn voice in his head—tossed her in his car and brought her home. Christ, the things he could be doing to her, right now...

Things you should be doing to me, but you let me down.

"Shut up!"

He turned as he reached into his pocket, tossing a salt bomb at Isabel's wavering spirit. It exploded in a circle of white as it hit the ground, the tiny flecks scattering in all directions. Isabel hissed then flickered, disappearing on a lingering scream.

He moved, grabbing a couple of tubs of salt out of the cupboard before heading for the front door. He ran a line along the floor, repeating the procedure at every window before making his way to the back. He ended with the French doors leading onto his back deck. He gave the rising full moon a passing glance as it glinted off the water, sparkling like a thousand diamonds across the calm surface before heading back to the kitchen. He rifled through a drawer, eventually finding the chalk he'd tucked away.

He made the rounds again, this time inscribing binding circles on the wooden floors. If the salt didn't stop her, he'd catch her ass once and for bloody all. White residue covered his denim when he stood before the rear doors, staring at the ancient marks, convinced he'd finally gone crazy. That he might not find his way back this time when the lights outside on the porch blinked. He waited, muscles tensed, gaze drifting toward his bag when the bulb flashed one more time then went out.

He released a weary breath. If that was the worst Isabel could do to him tonight, he'd consider it a win. He turned and walked over to the counter, placing the chalk on the surface. It rolled slightly then stopped, sitting there like a giant beacon, openly mocking him. He was a hunter, for god's sake. Surely, he could figure out how to rid himself of one ghost.

He waited for the telltale echo of Isabel's voice, letting his head bow forward when only the faint chirp of crickets sounded from outside. What if it all was in his head? If there was nothing haunting him but his own memories? Despite his reassurances that it was the fatigue, the stress —that it'd all fade once he'd finally forgiven himself—a part of him worried he'd never be able to put her to rest. That no amount of training would save him.

The porch floor creaked followed by the rattling of the door handle. Daniel fisted his hands on top of the counter, refusing to give her the satisfaction of turning. Of allowing her to see how much she affected him. Instead, he stood there, silently willing her to leave, when a swirl of air swept past his legs, the sounds of the forest increasing before shutting out, again.

Anger clawed at his resolve, finally breaking free. "For the last fucking time, Isabel, leave me the hell alone—"

His voice broke off as he spun, staring into a set of blue eyes. Drops of water clung to her skin, and he guessed it'd finally started raining. A rumble of thunder echoed overhead, shaking him free. He drew in a ragged breath, unsure whether to talk or just stand there, staring at the one woman who made him feel alive. Worthy.

Arrynn glanced around the room, carefully stepping over the marks on the floor without smudging them, as she closed the door and headed for him, stopping an arm's length away. She swept her gaze the length of him before settling on his face.

Hurt flashed in her eyes then vanished, the stone-cold operative looking back at him. "How long have you been seeing her?"

He raked a hand through his hair as he hissed out a breath. "Arrynn—"

"Stop fucking bullshitting me, and just answer the damn question! How long have you been seeing Isabel? It's been two years since we torched everything connected with her. She should be gone."

"You think I don't know that?" He laughed, the sound bitter. "You say it like I don't know how crazy this makes me look, which is why I never told you in the first place. I don't need you questioning my sanity. Trust me, I do it enough for both of us."

Arrynn slipped closer, her body nearly grazing his. "How long?"

He tempered the anger at the detached quality to her voice—as if he hadn't had his tongue down her throat less than an hour ago. His gaze dropped to her lips, his breath hitching at the fullness of them. The way they begged to be kissed, again.

The corners of her mouth lifted into the hint of a smile. "Daniel."

He forced himself to focus on her face—the rest of her face. "I heard her voice occasionally immediately after…"

Arrynn nodded. "Not unheard of. Probably just residual energy—a death echo of sorts. But it obviously turned into more if you're salting your damn entry points and drawing sigils on the floor."

He leaned fully against the counter, praying the slab would hold him up. Fuck, he was tired. Her hands landed on his chest, the palms pressing comfortingly against his torso. He gazed down at her, watching her eyes darken slightly as she eased her fingers up until she could thumb his cheeks.

She gave him a genuine smile, this time. "You said before that you care. So, talk to me."

He covered her hands with his, much like he'd done earlier. "A year ago today. That night I called and asked you to go for a drink. She'd appeared in the front room. I thought I was imagining it. That it was the guilt, the damn anniversary, but..."

Arrynn merely raised her brow when he didn't continue.

"But, she's been popping up more frequently, and not just here."

That brow furrowed as her eyes darted to the side, for a moment, before focusing on him, again. "Fuck. Today at the station. You *saw* her there, didn't you?"

She didn't wait for a reply, just spun and stormed away, heels clicking on his floor. She marched over to the rear window, fingering a bit of the salt before turning, again. "So...she was in the office?"

"And outside when we were..."

Arrynn cursed under her breath. "At least, it's comforting to know that it wasn't lack of desire that made you stop."

"You seriously thought I wasn't turned on? Fuck, Arrynn, I'm still hard. But feeling her touch my neck...

hearing her voice inside my head—"

"She touched you? Tonight? In the parking lot?"

"Yeah, so?" He stared as Arrynn darted toward him, grabbing him and spinning him around. "What the actual fuck, Arrynn?"

"I want to see if she marked you."

"There's nothing there. I already checked in the rearview." He glanced over his shoulder at her. "I know. Doesn't really give my claims any credence."

"It's not that I doubt you, it's just...you know as well as I do that ghosts can't simply pop up anywhere—"

"They're bound, to a place, a thing." He chuckled. "Go ahead. Say it. You think I'm crazy."

Her expression softened. "I think you're tired and feeling guilty because you feel responsible for Jimmy's death, even though there's no way you could have known."

"I should have broken the damn door down. I knew ditching the job—ditching me—was out of character."

"Daniel—"

"You would have gone inside."

She cringed at the hard tone in his voice. "You don't know that."

"Yes. I do."

She exhaled, taking a step back. "After everything that happened, we should err on the side of caution. We'll do a sweep of the house. Ensure nothing's inside. Then, we'll fortify the outer perimeter with silver dust. Moon's already up. And you look like you're about to fall over you're so exhausted."

"You don't look much better."

"Let's just say it's been a hell of a night, and it just

began. Thinking it'd be best if we both got some sleep... started fresh in the morning

"That sounds as if you're staying."

"Probably wise if you weren't alone...not if Isabel really is back."

"But you don't think she is."

She gave him a stunning smile that dropped his stomach and spiked his dick. "We'll figure it out. Promise. In the meantime..."

She walked past him, heading toward the front door, only to return with his bag. She dumped the contents, picking up a canister of silver powder. She handed it to him. "You go dust the ground. I'll do a sweep. If there's anything inside, I'll send it packing. That should secure the place, at least, for the night."

He accepted the container, inhaling as her fingers grazed his. Desire shot along his spine, and he had to bite back the moan that threatened to claw free. He hadn't gotten his need for her remotely out of his system, and with her staying the night...

Daniel eased past her, carefully stepping over the markings then heading outside. More thunder rumbled overhead followed by a flash of lightning as large drops splattered over his deck, leaving dark circles on the wood. He removed the cap on the canister, sprinkling a thin line along the perimeter of the cottage, some of the worry receding once he'd completed a circle. Arrynn was waiting for him when he stepped back inside, shaking the rain off his jacket.

She motioned to the tub. "All set?"

"Dusting the ground isn't exactly rocket science, so yeah...mission accomplished." He moved in beside her, placing the canister on the counter. "Everything okay in here?"

"A few residual spikes in the living room, but nothing to suggest there's anyone else here with us. Couldn't help but notice you used a salt bomb in there. Thinking that sent our friend packing. And, with these added precautions…should be a relatively uneventful night."

He couldn't stop his lips from lifting. Nothing about tonight was going to be uneventful—not if he had a say. He shuffled closer. "So…you don't need anything from your car?"

"Like what? My makeup bag? I'm good. All I need is a place to crash." She motioned to the living room. "Can I borrow your sofa for the next several hours?"

He snagged her wrist. "Do you really think you're getting anywhere near that couch? After what happened tonight?"

"What happened tonight? You mean the part where you kissed me then basically said I was a mistake you'd regret."

He cringed slightly at the hurt tone of her voice. He knew she'd be pissed—he just hoped he could convince her to forgive him. "I never said…" He sighed. "You're right. I acted like an ass, and I'm sorry—not that words make it okay. But, in my defense, hearing Isabel taunt me, then seeing her… I was afraid if I told you the truth, you'd kick me out of the program. Or lock me up in a padded room."

Her expression softened slightly. "Now, that's crazy talk."

"I just didn't want to disappoint you."

Her body tensed, her breathing roughening. "Never.

But we both know part of this is a byproduct of losing Jimmy. Wanting to hold on to what we have left."

He closed the scant distance between them, palming her hips. "Maybe. Or maybe I'm just tired of fighting this. Pretending you don't make me wish for so much more. So, if you don't feel the same…"

The rest of his words faded into the firm press of her mouth against his as she stepped into him, hands landing on his chest as she tugged him close. She brushed her mouth over his, smiling at his muffled moan.

"About time you came to your senses." She eased back when he moved to kiss her. "But know this… Once we cross this line, there's no going back."

"Oh, sweetheart. If we're going to burn a bridge, let's make the fire big enough it'll light our way."

CHAPTER FIVE

Arrynn inhaled as Daniel slanted his mouth over hers, this kiss more demanding than the one in the parking lot. Warm, musky spice filled her senses, his taste matching the underlying scent of his skin. And god, she'd spent the past two years wrapped in that scent. Having it work its way onto her clothes until she could still smell his essence long after they'd parted.

Her fingers tightened around his jacket as his hands smoothed along her back, one staying low as the other traced her spine before burying in her hair. His fingers flexed then released, the pressure making her inhale. She shoved her hands to the side, jerking his jacket off his shoulders, but the bugger didn't release her so she could push it off. Instead, he dragged her hips closer as he tilted her head back.

His mouth blazed a path down her neck, his breath cooling her suddenly heated flesh. "Impatient, aren't you?"

Her grip faltered slightly as he nipped at her shoulder

muscle through her shirt. "I've already waited an obscene amount of time to get to this point. And we both know patience isn't my strong suit."

Daniel sighed, finally easing back. "I'm trying to be romantic."

"Romance my ass, next time."

The muscle in his jaw jumped, his pupils widening until they'd nearly eclipsed the blue.

She tiptoed up, catching his bottom lip between her teeth before licking it. "I don't want soft and gentle. Not tonight. Not when I'm barely hanging on by a thread. You said earlier you wanted to forget. Let's forget together. Lose that precious control of yours. Make it impossible for either of us to think about anything other than how hard you're fucking me."

"Shit." He claimed her mouth, again, holding her close as he somehow maneuvered them down the adjoining hallway, bouncing into a few walls in the process, until they reached his room. His breathing kicked up as he released her, moving away enough to shuck his jacket then toe off his shoes. He took a predatory step forward, his fingers already working the button on his jeans. "Two options. Either you strip, or some of your clothes don't hit the floor in one piece. Your choice, sweetheart."

His words made her body cream in anticipation as she tossed her shirt on the ground, lowering her hands to her jeans. She'd only gotten them partway off when he tsked.

He stepped out of his jeans. "Option two it is."

"But—"

Her voice cut off as he grabbed her, carrying her across the room then tossing her onto his bed. She bounced once before he was on top of her, his body pinning her down as he took her mouth. His tongue swept inside as one hand cupped her ass.

She arched into him, not willing to back down, as she sank her fingers into his hair, anchoring him to her. God, she loved that his hair was slightly longer. That she could wrap the strands around her fingers—use the thick mass as a way of grounding herself when her body clearly wanted to fly apart. And all he'd done was kiss her.

Daniel hummed after he'd released her lips, once again kissing a line down her neck. "Fuck, you taste good. And your skin…" He nuzzled the soft spot at the base of her neck. "It's like silk."

He pushed off of her, standing with her knees wedged around his as he grabbed one leg, straightening it before removing her boot. He tossed it over his shoulder, tugging off her sock then did the same to the other side, pausing to massage her foot.

She moaned, allowing her head to fall into the mattress. "Was there something wrong with the way I was stripping?"

"Too slow. You can't taunt me to lose control then expect me to wait."

He grabbed her pants, pulling the denim the rest of the way off before tossing it aside. Then, he snagged her G-string, tearing the small elastic bands at each side. The sound made her stomach flutter as her pussy clenched, moisture easing out to coat her cleft.

"Had to hold true to my promise, sweetheart, lest you think I'm not a man of my word." He winked at her. "Figured you could live without the panties."

She stared at him, her gaze dropping to his briefs…the only stitch of clothing he had left. "I'm not the only one still wearing clothing, though you look as if you might punch through those shorts at any moment."

"Your fault entirely. You're too damn sexy for your own good." He gave her a wicked smile, batting away her hand when she reached for him. "Not until I've finished undressing you."

"I thought this was about getting to the main course as quickly as possible?"

"So did I, until just now, when I realized I like the view. Like watching you respond to me. The way your skin flushes then beads in anticipation. How I can barely see the blue in your eyes." He shrugged. "I'm man enough to admit when I'm wrong, and thinking this would be a quick fuck... Yeah, that was one of those mistakes I mentioned earlier."

Arrynn bit back the moan that rumbled around her chest. "Christ. Keep talking like that, and this will be over before you even get inside me."

"Telling me you might come isn't a threat, Arrynn. More like an inevitability."

She pressed her head into the mattress, trying not to focus on the slow slide of his hands along her thighs, lightly brushing her pussy before continuing upward. On the way, he traced her ribs as he moved along her torso, teasing her nipples through her bra. He nipped at the taut peaks, smiling as they poked against the cotton.

"So pretty. I wonder if they're the same shade of pink as your lips?"

He wrapped one arm around her back, levering her onto her ass. His hands grabbed the bottom of her bra, lifting it over her head. "Almost, but not quite."

She shivered at the sudden curl of the cool air against her heated flesh.

Daniel frowned. "Everything okay?"

He glanced over his shoulder, but she drew his chin back with a single finger.

"Just because I shiver doesn't mean there's a ghost in the room." She skimmed her hands down his ribcage to the waistband of his shorts. "Now, since I'm naked, I figure it's my turn." She slipped her fingers under the edge of his briefs before tugging them down. "Damn."

His gaze focused on her as his cock sprang free. A line of pre-cum glistened from his shaft to his stomach, the strand wavering for a few moments before snapping. The moan that rumbled through her chest made him smile as his fingers sank into her hair, again.

He traced the pad of his thumb over her bottom lip. "God, no matter how many times I've envisioned you like this—hair messed, your body quivering with anticipation. I never thought you'd look at me like that."

She cocked an eyebrow. "Like what?"

"As if I was the answer to all those questions inside your head."

"Only the important ones." She reached for him, smiling when he didn't stop her fingers from encircling his cock. "I've always wondered if you'd feel half as good in my mouth as I imagined. Thinking it's time I found out." She leaned in then paused. "Unless you had other plans?"

The muscle in his jaw jumped, again. "If I did, I'll change them, because just thinking about you putting your lips on me... Christ."

His body tensed as she blew a heated breath across the

flared head, flicking out her tongue to lick away the new bead of fluid. Salty spice burst in her mouth, the flavor matching his scent. She eased back, caressing the silky skin with her index finger.

"Fuck, Daniel." She bathed the entire crown this time, nipping at the end before pulling away, again. "God, you feel good against my tongue." She made another pass, humming along his length, loving the way his body jerked at the small vibrations. Christ, she could do this for hours. Watch him unravel over and over, knowing it was her touch that drove him past his limits.

Daniel's grip tightened, and she paused, waiting to see if he'd make her stop, only to moan when his other hand cupped her jaw, his finger tracing where her lips touched his shaft. "Fuck, sweetheart. Seeing your pretty mouth stretched around me. Damn, I won't last long this way."

She bobbed down, sucking her way back up before popping him free. "Isn't that the point?"

His brow furrowed. "I have more than a few things I want to do to you before I come like a damn teenager on the first pass."

A smile teased her lips. "Are you only good for one climax? Figured you more for the fast-recovery type."

The brow lifted into an arch. "Are you seriously challenging me, again? Dangerous."

"Only if you can't walk the walk, baby."

The fingers in her hair flexed, the muscles in his abdomen tensing. "Take me deep."

She grinned then leaned forward, again, teasing his shaft with rapid flicks of her tongue before sealing her lips around the head and slowly taking him inside. His cock thickened, the head flaring as she stopped with him lodged in her throat. His fingers twitched in her hair, the slight sting making her inhale through her nose before she eased back, bathing the head, again, as he slipped free.

Daniel moaned, the raspy sound going straight to her pussy. It clenched emptily, her stomach flip-flopping in anticipation. She focused on his shaft, repeating the deep caress, loving the way his entire body seemed to react. His thighs and abdomen flexed, the muscles clenching then releasing as his fingers followed suit. She glanced up, smiling inwardly as his head tilted back, the lines in his neck cording.

God, she loved seeing him like this. On the edge, his body strung tight. Knowing he was only a few minutes away from shooting down her throat. And she wanted him to. Wanted him to surrender to her—allow himself to be vulnerable as she swallowed every damn drop.

Her pussy contracted, again, making her whimper ever so softly. Daniel tugged on her hair, gaining her attention. He arched a brow in question. She made a few more passes before releasing him.

He thumbed her mouth. "You okay?"

"If you call be needy as fuck, okay...then yes."

He grinned. "Oh, you'll be full of me before the night's out. I promise you that."

Another fucking empty clench. "Not helping, Daniel."

"Then, get up off your knees and put your ass on the bed."

"Before you give me what I want? I don't think so."

"Arrynn..."

His voice trailed into a moan, his eyes squeezing shut as she took him deep, doing her best to swallow with his cock still lodged in her mouth. His hips bucked forward, a husky rasp rumbling from his chest.

The sound settled in her core, heating her from the inside out. This is how she wanted him. Desperate. Ready to explode at the next deep plunge of her mouth. She eased back, keeping the head inside before sinking down his length, again.

"Shit, so damn good." He thrust slightly, seemingly warring with letting her lead and wanting to pound into her mouth. "God, you undo me."

She made a few more passes, huffing at how he pulled himself back. She eased his cock free, still working his erection with her hand. "I said I needed you to lose control. I want you to fuck my mouth. Show me how you plan on claiming the rest of me."

His gaze snapped down to hers, the look in his eyes nothing short of feral. She held his focus, arching her brow before sinking along his length. His fingers fisted around her strands before he sighed. His shoulders drooped in seeming defeat a moment before he began moving—matching each downward plunge of her mouth with a firm upward stroke. His cock hit the back of her throat, but she didn't ask him to stop—reveling in his loss of composure. In the way his hands held her head still, aligning her mouth with his pistoning shaft. How his muscles quivered, creating shadows along his skin.

His breathing rasped through the room, the rough quality making her pussy cream. "Fuck, sweetheart. I'm close. Won't be able to hold off much longer. If you don't want me to shoot this down your throat, then back off."

She glared at him, at least she hoped that was the expression as she paused for a few heartbeats, staring up at him, her hand wrapped around the base as she kept him deep inside her mouth.

Daniel inhaled roughly then nodded. "Shit, you win. God, so good. So damn hot." He started moving in earnest, fucking her mouth with long, punishing strokes. "You want me to come? Fill you until you'll be able to taste me tomorrow?"

His voice became a strangled grunt as his head tipped back, again, his body starting to shake. He made several more passes before moaning her name as his cock thickened in her mouth, the end flaring wide.

"Christ, now, sweetheart. Yes!"

Bitter musk filled her senses as he exploded, sending spurt after spurt of fluid down her throat. She swallowed, pumping him until his fingers fell from her hair as he curled over her, his cock softening slightly. She smiled, slowly drawing down his length before allowing him to slip free. A shiver shook through him, and she dropped a kiss on his hip, pressing her cheek against his lower abdomen. The muscles twitched from the contact, a shaky breath sounding above her.

His hands fell to her shoulders, slipping under her arms before helping her to her feet. She opened for his tongue when his mouth landed on hers, this kiss more playful than the others. As if she'd eased some of the burden she knew he carried around with him like a shield. A way of remaining emotionally detached. Clinical.

One hand stroked her hair, his breath raking over her skin. "Fuck, Arrynn. While I'll chalk it up to your mastery of oral sex...can't help but feel a bit disappointed I came that hard, that fast."

She chuckled. "Not sure how you're seeing that as a loss in any form."

"The only loss was my control. You... You're nothing short of an epic win. But it does bring up the fact that I let you have your way."

"Let? Me?"

He pulled back enough to show her the smirk on his face. "Damn, I love that you're so easy to rile. The point is... It's my turn. And I won't consider my pride truly restored until you scream so loud the damn windows rattle." He shoved her back, grinning when her ass landed on the bed. "Get comfortable, because I plan on having my tongue buried in your cleft for the foreseeable future."

CHAPTER SIX

Daniel splayed his hands along Arrynn's thighs, smiling as her breath hitched, the blue in her eyes fading into lust-blown pupils. Her muscles jumped at the light contact as he slowly inched his hands up her legs, stopping when his thumbs brushed along the edges of her pussy. Warm moisture slicked across her skin, the sweet scent of her arousal making him hum.

He shook his head. "Damn, sweetheart. I haven't even touched you, yet, and you're already soaking." He swirled his thumbs inward, tracing the smooth inner flesh of her folds. "Christ. So damn hot and wet. Can't wait to have you cream my tongue."

A strangled rasp rumbled from her chest, the gravelly sound making his cock throb, hardening it. At this rate, he'd be ready and aching, again, before she'd screamed her first release. He smiled at the thought, teasing her slit with one hand as he leaned forward, hovering over her. She stared up at him, reaching for his shoulders. He moved with her when she pulled him down, her mouth claiming his.

He savored the tangle of her tongue with his, sensing she needed the contact to stay grounded. To keep her emotions somewhat in check. Or maybe, he was the one who needed it. Who felt as if he'd simply break apart without her holding him. Without her fingers digging into his flesh as her body quivered in anticipation.

Daniel nipped at her neck once she'd released him, tasting the slightly salty perfection of her skin, already aware tonight wouldn't be enough. That no matter how many times they made love, he'd need more. More flesh, more friction, more *her*.

He sighed inwardly. Now wasn't the time to fill up his head with romantic sentiments. Though he was crazy about Arrynn, he knew what she'd said was right. A large part of this was a byproduct of losing Jimmy. A way of replacing the pain with pleasure. Thinking this was the beginning of forever would only complicate things afterward. And, regardless of what happened next, they were partners. The last thing he needed was to ruin any chance at working together.

She tensed beneath him, her fingers grazing his arm, drawing his attention. "You okay?"

He smiled. "Fuck, you're beautiful."

She snorted. "I saw that look on your face, Daniel. You weren't with me." She snagged her lower lip. "If you're having second thoughts—"

"Hell, no. All my thoughts, second and otherwise, are on you. It's just... I can't stop thinking that it could have been you today. That I could have lost *you*." He swallowed against the lump in his throat. "Shit, Arrynn. I don't know what...

Her expression softened. "Kiss me."

He dipped down, taking her mouth, letting himself drown in her. In her taste, her skin, her hands on his back. In the way she made everything else vanish. Made everything right. Her breath skirted along his jaw as he eased back, allowing his forehead to rest on hers. Her fingers dug into his flesh, the firm pressure making him smile.

He stayed close, kissing and licking his way down her neck to her chest, nuzzling the soft inner curve of her breasts. They weren't overly large, the slightly rounded mounds matching her athletic frame, but they were more than tempting. He skimmed across to her nipple, watching it crinkle against her skin. He flicked his tongue across the tip, rewarded with a sharp inhale as her fingers flexed against his back. He repeated the process, nipping the end, this time.

He switched sides, teasing her other breast, savoring the way her entire body reacted. How she tightened her grip, her nails scoring his skin. How her chest heaved beneath his mouth, her roughened pants jacking up his desire. The wet evidence of her need slicking his thigh as she ground her pussy against his leg.

Arrynn tugged on his hair, her murmured pleas making him smile against her skin before he finally moved down, dipping his tongue into her bellybutton. She twitched, laughing at the contact before her voice morphed into a throaty moan as he nuzzled the top of her mound. Warm, sweet spice filled his senses, and he inched lower, needing a truer taste.

"God, Daniel…"

Her voice faded, the words becoming nothing more than soft moans as he swept his tongue through her slit, flicking it across her clit. Her hips arched in response, her thighs opening wider in invitation. He accepted, slipping his hands under her ass as he lifted her against his mouth, licking at the arousal that coated her silky flesh.

He hummed, loving the way the tiny vibrations drew a strangled cry from her. "So fucking sweet. Damn, I could lick you for hours."

"Seconds. You have seconds left before I come."

He chuckled. "Then, I suppose I'll have to make the most of that small amount of time. Or maybe I should stop—"

"No."

He eased back, ignoring her huff of protest or how her fingers tightened in his hair. "Don't you want this to last longer?"

"Next time. You can tease me longer, next time."

He smiled at the thought. Hell yeah, there'd be a next time. And another dozen after that. He pushed his thumb forward, sinking it inside her passage, smiling as her breath caught as her eyes rolled back a bit. "Fine. I'll give in to your demands, this time. Now, be a good girl and grind your pussy on my face as I make you scream."

He dipped down, burying his face in her cleft. His tongue lapped at her clit as he pumped his hand, taking her pussy in steady strokes. Arrynn moaned his name, pressing her groin against his face, practically rubbing herself off on him. He nipped at her clit, sucking it as he added another finger, his other hand palming her breast.

He pinched at her nipple, not hard but enough to draw a strangled cry from her as a rush of juice coated her folds.

He moved back a bit, watching his fingers slide in and out of her hole, slick and shiny with her arousal. A deep flush covered her chest and neck as the muscles in her stomach and thighs flexed. He rolled her nipple, timing the pressure with a firm thrust. Her body stiffened, a murmured plea lighting the air.

He moaned. "What was that, sweetheart? I didn't quite hear you."

She grunted, pushing onto her elbows, only to collapse back when he repeated the action. "Christ, Daniel, just... please. I'm so close."

"We'll have to work on your patience, but since you asked so nicely."

He attacked her clit, knowing she was too close for more teasing. And he'd be damned if he was going to miss the chance to taste her release. Feel her flesh contract around him as she climaxed. Arrynn arched into him, thighs clenching around his shoulders as her body seemed to hover on the edge before tumbling over.

"Yes! Daniel, god..."

His name became a wash of mumbled words he couldn't make out as she spasmed around him, her pussy rippling around his fingers as her release slicked her folds. He closed his eyes, licking at the flesh, humming his approval until she moaned, and her thighs fell to the mattress.

He gave her nub one last open-mouthed kiss before moving to his feet. He stared down at her, lost in the way she still writhed on the bed, the last remnants of her orgasm twitching her muscles. He reached for the side table when her hand snagged his. He looked at her, brow arched in question.

She wet her lips, eyes still lust-blown. Her gaze darted to the table then back. She seemed to war with some kind of internal battle before huffing. "I'm on the pill."

His pulsed kicked up. Damn, was she suggesting... "Are you asking me to go bareback?"

Crimson bloomed in her cheeks before she shook her head. "Forget it, I just thought..."

Fire licked along his skin as his vision seemed to narrow until nothing but the mixed emotions on her face seemed to register. He clenched his jaw, gathering some semblance of control before moving over her. "We've trusted each other with our lives for the past two years. Seems only fitting we continue that here, don't you think?"

Her smile dropped his stomach as he went to his elbows, forcing her to smooth her hands around to his back. Her fingers dug in, again, the firm pressure grounding him. He thrust forward, burying himself completely inside her. The hot slide of skin on skin sent a rush of fire straight to his sac, and he had to clench his abdomen to keep from coming. Arrynn gasped, her eyes drifting shut as her pussy spasmed around his length, another rush of fluid heating his shaft.

He mouthed her neck, biting at the strong muscle threading into her shoulder. "Did you just come? Again? Oh, sweetheart, it's going to be a long night for you."

He started pumping, doing everything he could to ignore the slick glide of her flesh against his. How it felt hotter, wetter. How every pass fluttered her walls along his cock, threatening to unhinge him. Arrynn wrapped her legs around his back, meeting every thrust, taking him deeper.

He gritted his teeth. "Shit, sweetheart. I'm not going to last long if you keep..." His voice trailed into a grunt when she squeezed around him.

She nipped at his ear. "Long, short. All I need is you. In me. With me."

"Christ." He levered back, breaking her hold. "Knees. Now."

He didn't wait for her to comply, simply grabbed her and tossed her over. He thought he heard her giggle, but it was drowned out by the pounding of his pulse in his head. By the feel of her muscles beneath his fingers, the smooth caress of her skin against his. While a part of him wanted to stay poised over her. Watch her face as she climaxed. He needed more. Needed her to surrender to him.

He grunted as Arrynn shifted into place, her thighs splayed around his, her back flexing as she glanced over her shoulder at him. A knowing smile tilted her lips, and he couldn't stop from smacking her ass. Not hard. Just enough to make it shimmy from the force—add a hint of pink color to her skin. Her eyes closed at the contact, the muscle in her jaw jumping before she gazed at him, again, even less of the blue ring visible.

He smoothed his hand over her ass. "Damn, you've got an amazing rear end." He trailed a single finger down her crease, circling her tight pucker. When she pushed into his touch, he teased the hole, sinking just the tip inside. "I can't wait to take you here. Feel you clench around me. See how hard you come. How loud you'll scream my name."

"Yes, shit, anything, just do *something*."

He chuckled. "We really need to work on your patience, sweetheart."

"Patience is for talkers. Fucking is for people of action." She arched her brow. "Was I wrong? Are you *not* a man of action, Daniel?"

"Goading me to get what you want? That, I didn't see coming. But your tactics won't work. My pace..." He eased back when she pushed against his hand, again. "Or shall I stop?"

"Fuck, Daniel!" She sighed as he removed his finger, her head bowing toward her chest. "Fine. You can be in control, just...don't stop. God, please, don't stop. I need..."

Her breath hitched into a gasp as he pushed into her, claiming her pussy in one hard stroke. Her back strained as her head flew up, her hair spilling over her shoulders.

Daniel slid his hand along her spine, feeling her body twitch and flex before burying his fingers in her hair. He eased his other hand forward off her hip, anchoring it on her chest as he used both holds to lever her upright, lock her head next to his collarbone.

"Yeah." He tightened his hold, surrounding her with his body. "This is how I want you. Firm against me, completely open for me."

She whimpered as he pounded into her, keeping her still as his hips slapped her ass, plunging him deep. Her channel rippled around his shaft, each thrust echoed by a throaty affirmation. Her hands latched onto his arm, nails biting in as she screamed his name, pussy contracting hard around his cock.

"That's it, sweetheart. Come all over me. Not done, yet."

He kept moving, her hot, wet release only increasing the burning need in his gut. He shuffled them forward on the bed until she palmed the wall as he pinned her chest against it, shifting his arm down to cup her mound. He v'ed his fingers around his shaft as it pumped into her, her juice coating his skin.

Daniel bit at her earlobe, breathing harshly across her neck. "God, Arrynn, what you do to me. I want to possess you. Fucking crawl up inside of you and feel you explode from the inside out." He angled his hips differently, rubbing her g-spot with every pass.

"Oh, god. Now. So damn much."

Her words were followed by a hissing cry as she climaxed, again, her body convulsing within his embrace. Daniel bowed his head to her neck, knowing he wouldn't be able to hold off. Not with her juice heating his shaft, the smell of her release surrounding him in a lusty haze. He held her firm, thumbing her clit as he let himself go.

He pounded into her, bed creaking, headboard banging the wall. She stiffened, again, another set of contractions taking him over. The tingling sensation in his balls shot forward, pulsing his cock until he emptied inside her, the tight clasp of her pussy stealing his breath. He held himself rigid, hips grinding into her ass until his strength waned, and he curled over her, head pressed to her back, sweat beading both of their bodies. Arrynn shivered, the tiny vibrations shaking away some of the fogginess.

Out of habit, he glanced around the room, half expecting to see Isabel's ghostly form hovering nearby. But the room was empty, nothing but their ragged breathing sounding within the space. Daniel tried to slow the frantic inhalations, holding Arrynn close as he came back down. She seemed boneless in his arms when he was finally coherent enough to straighten.

Her hands clasped his arm as it settled between her breasts, again, her grip noticeably weaker. "Don't go."

He smiled against her hair, dropping a kiss on her shoulder. "Not going anywhere. But I need to get a cloth...clean us both up. I promise, I'll only be a moment."

She glanced at him as he eased free, a disappointed sigh following his departure. He kissed her quick, motioning her to stay as he darted to the bathroom and warmed the water. He rinsed himself off then wet a cloth, ensuring it was hot enough before heading back. She'd managed to slide onto her butt, back resting against the headboard as he crossed the short space. She didn't speak as he opened her thighs, gently dabbing away the evidence of their combined release.

He stared at the cloth, part of him wishing he could just leave his seed coating her thighs. Proof to anyone she was his, even if it was only for tonight. The thought soured his stomach as he finished cleaning her skin then tossed the rag toward the bathroom. It fell wetly to the floor just inside the door, but damn, it was close enough for him.

Arrynn nudged him. "Won't that ruin your floor?"

"Have to redo those ones, anyway. Besides, holding you is more important."

Her chin quivered a bit before she reached for his neck, tugging him in for a punishing kiss. He let her lead, knowing she needed the roughness to pull back—hide away the emotions she'd exposed.

She seemed more reserved when she eased back. "You are so much more than I ever anticipated."

"I'm not the only one, sweetheart. You…" He sighed. "You're dangerous. Now, scoot your butt down. I'm exhausted. You can seek your revenge in the morning."

"Revenge? I like the sound of that."

She shuffled over, resting her head on his chest when he reclined beside her. She sighed, palming his chest. "Thanks."

"For what?"

"For making me feel human tonight. Helping me forget."

"My pleasure." He kissed the top of her head. "Sleep. We'll deal with the real world tomorrow. Figure all this shit out—just know this…" He tilted her chin up with a gentle finger. "Not going to let anything happen to you."

She punched him in the chest. "I'm not fragile, jackass. Pretty damn sure I've saved your ass a time or two."

"You have…though that does remind me…"

She arched a brow at his silence.

"I have big plans for your ass. So, you'd better rest up."

Arrynn shook her head, settling in. Her breathing slowed almost immediately, her limbs going limp. Daniel held her close, listening to her soft inhalations. He meant what he'd said. Nothing was going to touch her except him. And, if that meant he had to exorcise every damn ghost for a hundred miles, he'd do it. Arrynn was his.

CHAPTER SEVEN

Mine.

Arrynn blinked, opening her eyes as the soft voice faded into the scuff of feet across the wood floors, the sound drifting in from the kitchen. She glanced at the window, noting the splash of sunlight around the edge of the curtains. It was obviously past sunrise, though she couldn't quite remember falling asleep on Daniel's couch, not that she was surprised. It'd been a week since they'd lost Jimmy—since they'd crossed the line from partners to lovers—and they'd barely slept since. Between trying to piece together Jimmy's last few months and working other cases, they'd gone three days on coffee and sugar.

She laid her arm over her forehead. Seven damn days and not a single lead into who or what had killed their partner. Tanner had called Barry for the last few days, trying to get Jimmy's personal effects sent over to the center, but had only gotten more excuses. Workload issues, a backup in the morgue—it all meant the same thing. Waiting.

An uneasy feeling churned in her gut, though she wasn't sure if it was the case or the fact she and Daniel hadn't managed to squeeze in a minute of alone time since their one romp between the sheets. They'd either been hunting spirits or scouring through phone records and old files.

She groaned inwardly, aware it wasn't the lack of physical contact that seemed to be slowly eating a hole in her stomach, but the doubt. The gnawing uncertainty that making love to her had ended up being a mistake Daniel regretted, and he just hadn't thought of a suitable way to tell her. It didn't help that their encounter had haunted her thoughts for the past week. That she couldn't look at him without imagining his fingers caressing her skin. How he felt moving within her. The raspy timbre of his voice when he'd shouted her name as he'd emptied inside her.

Christ. This was exactly why she never should have crossed that line. She'd had feelings for him since he'd joined the unit. Becoming lovers had increased those feelings tenfold. Hell, she was pretty damn sure she loved the man. She just wished she knew if he felt the same. If his skin itched to touch hers. If he feared he was, also, slowly going insane trying to puzzle it all out. Of course, the fact he hadn't carried her to his bed didn't bode well.

"That's a pretty intense frown for just waking up."

She glanced toward the kitchen just as Daniel stopped beside the couch, two mugs in hand. He gave her a brilliant smile as he sat beside her.

"I heard you shuffling about. Thought you might need this." He handed her one of the cups. "Black, two sugars."

She accepted the mug, taking a cautious sip. "Damn,

this is good." She motioned toward the window. "What time is it?"

"Nearly two."

She coughed, choking on her coffee. "Two? Shit, why the hell did you let me sleep that long?"

"We didn't get in until four this morning after thirty-six hours straight. That's not that long."

"We have work to do."

"Killing ourselves won't solve Jimmy's case." He reached forward, tucking some of her hair behind her ear. "And, in case you're wondering, I didn't move you to my bed because I fell asleep in the damn chair as quickly as you passed out on the couch. My neck's going to hurt for days."

She tensed. "I didn't expect..."

He chuckled as he silenced her with a finger across her lips. "I'm not the only one who's a terrible liar."

He leaned in, licking a path across her lower lip before sealing his mouth to hers. His tongue swept inside, the flavor of coffee and warm male essence mixing together. She returned his intensity, somewhat surprised the damn cup didn't tip once he eased back, nuzzling her nose as he stayed no more than a breath away.

"God, I've missed touching you. Seems there hasn't been a spare minute since we got rudely called back in. But it wasn't for lack of wanting you." He stood. "Don't suppose you'd like to join me in the shower?"

Her breath hitched as a slow smile spread across her face.

He grinned. "I'll take that as a yes."

He dipped down, gathering her in his arms. She

wrapped her hands around his neck, laughing as he picked her up then headed for the back of the house.

"I can walk, Daniel."

"I know."

She laughed inwardly, laying her head against his chest when he just kept going. She had to admit there was something inherently intimate about having him carry her, even if the action was more likely a result of his stubbornness than anything else. Still, it made her feel cherished.

He maneuvered them down the hallway and through his bedroom, finally placing her on her feet in front of the shower. He motioned for her to stay put with his finger as he reached in and turned on the shower, the instant patter of water against the tiles filling the room.

Arrynn smiled when a cool breeze swirled around her feet. She glanced toward the doorway, inhaling when the faint reflection of a white dress faded amidst the rising steam. She took a step forward when Daniel grabbed her arm, again.

He looked at the doorway then back at her. "Arrynn? Everything okay?"

She blinked, half wondering if she'd even seen the ghostly image or if it had merely been an illusion wrought from steam, weariness, and a healthy dose of paranoia. She turned her attention to him. "Fine, I just..." She waved her hand. "I'm sure it's nothing."

He frowned. "We both know better than to brush something off as our imagination. What did you think you saw? I know you better than you want to believe, and I've seen that expression before. You get it when we're hunting."

She blew out her next breath. "I stand by my previous claim. You're a pain in the ass." She sighed. "But...I thought I saw something by the door."

He looked at the area, again. "What was it?"

"Just a lingering image, but I swear it was a white dress."

Daniel's body tensed, his grip tightening slightly. "Anything else?"

She tugged on his arm, gaining his attention. "I know what you're thinking but...there's no reason to believe it's Isabel. Hell, I've been at your side nonstop this past week. There hasn't been a hint of her since that night."

"You still think it's all in my head—hearing her. Seeing her."

It wasn't a question, and she hated the way he steeled himself against her reply, hiding behind the walls she desperately wanted to knock down permanently.

"I didn't say that." She huffed at his blank expression. "Can we not argue the first chance we get to play around? That *is* why you asked me to join you, right? So, you could take delicious advantage of me? After all, I believe you'd promised me a 'next time'. Wouldn't want you to go back on your word."

His eyes darkened at her words, his gaze drifting along the length of her. He nodded, stepping against her. "You're right. Everything else can wait. Which means you're terribly overdressed."

He reached for her, shucking her clothes before removing his. He grabbed her hand, leading her into the stall. Water sluiced over her skin before he tugged her hard against him as his mouth came down on hers, his tongue slipping inside.

Arrynn gave herself over to the kiss, inhaling when he pinned her against the cool tiles. Even with the warm steam, the slight chill stole her breath, the sensation intensified by the hot press of his body against her front. She raked her hands through his wet strands, holding him tight against her as he finally broke the kiss, licking his way down her neck.

He hummed, nipping at her shoulder. "Damn, I've missed you."

"Didn't we just establish I haven't left your side all week?"

"Not the same as having you like this. Touching. Holding. It's all I've thought about." He straightened, still pinning her to the wall. "Need you."

She replied with a nod, afraid her voice would crack at the desperation in his eyes. Christ, she'd never witnessed him show such raw emotion before. As if his sanity, his worth, depended on their coming together. On how loud she screamed his name. How many times she pulsed around him.

If Daniel sensed the rawness coursing through her, he didn't say anything, choosing to wrap her around him as he lifted her slightly, aligning her pussy with his cock. The head nudged her sex, the slippery skin giving way as he slid her onto him, locking her groin to his. Her head fell back against the tiles, a guttural moan filling the small space.

His breath sounded beside her ear, the rough quality making her stomach flutter. "Christ, you're wet. So damn hot and tight."

He eased back, pausing with just the head locked inside her before bottoming out, again—slapping her back against the wall. She cinched her arms around his neck, levering her crossed heels on the small of his back as he pounded into her, deflecting the spray against the glass door with every thrust. Fire swirled through her abdomen, quickly culminating into a hard climax as he grazed her g-spot, his chest rubbing across her sensitive nipples. Heat billowed up from beneath her, sending her crashing over as he somehow went deeper, filling her until she thought she'd split apart.

"Oh, hell yeah. Come for me, Arrynn. That's my girl. Just keep coming."

He increased his pace, shafting her faster, never allowing her to descend. She crested into another release, her nails scoring his back as the intense sensation threatened to pull her under. Black dots flickered along the edge of her vision before she squeezed shut her eyes, nothing registering but his body slamming into her.

Daniel shifted, keeping her pressed into the wall while managing to wedge his hand between them—pinch her clit as he lowered his head and bit her nipple.

"Fuck!"

She convulsed around him, coming so hard a dull roaring sounded in her ears. She thought he shouted her name—felt his cock empty in her pulsing channel—but it blurred into the beat of his heart syncing with hers. Time seemed to slow until nothing but the steady splash of water against her skin made it beyond the darkness.

Daniel's heartbeat thrashing against her chest finally roused her, and she managed to open her eyes. His head rested next to hers, his breath coasting over her skin. God, she'd never had a lover claim her like that—completely.

Almost brutally. She let her head connect with his shoulder, her teeth nipping at his muscles.

He chuckled, drawing a ragged breath before lifting his head. Lust-filled eyes stared back at her, the thin ring of blue making her smile. He tsked. "I know that look, too, but no more sex for you until we take care of some other needs. I'm starving."

"You're the one who doesn't seem to know how to pace themselves."

He shrugged. "Why save something for later when you're only guaranteed this moment?"

The odd tone to his voice drew her attention, and she held his gaze as he eased her feet to the floor, slowly pulling out of her.

She smoothed her hands to his face, cupping each side. "Are we still talking about sex? Because it doesn't seem like it."

He sighed, kissing each palm before stepping back, emotionally distancing himself, again.

She raked her hand through her hair, pushing back the wet strands, wishing she'd just kept her mouth shut. "Look, if this is happening too fast, or too soon..."

Daniel balked, staring at her as if she'd grown a set of horns. "Is that what you think? That my seeing Isabel is because I'm still hopelessly in love with her?"

"I just want you to know, I understand."

"God, you couldn't be more wrong."

He spun, fisting the handle to the door when she snagged his wrist, preventing him from opening the glass panel.

She used a slight arm lock to pivot his back against the wall before moving into his personal space. "Don't. Don't you fucking walk out on me because talking hurts. We're both hurting. But you don't get to use it as an excuse to run from me. Scream. Rant. Do whatever you need to, but you'll fucking face me."

Daniel's jaw twitched a moment before he moved, using his strength to spin her against the wall, again. Her breath caught at the way he stared at her—eyes dark. Color high on his cheeks. He tunneled his fingers through her hair, taking her mouth in a brutal kiss before laying his forehead on hers, drinking in her frantic breath. The fight seemed to drain out of him, leaving a side of the man she'd never seen before.

He brushed his thumb along her cheek, lightly caressing her lips. "I'm not running from you. Not you."

She cupped his face, again, waiting until he met her gaze. "Nothing you say is going to alter my perception of you. You know that, right?"

"You sure about that?"

"Pretty damn sure."

He sighed, dropping a soft kiss on her mouth before stepping back. He turned off the water, then stepped out, grabbing a towel. He tossed one to her when she followed him out, leaning against the far wall. He scrubbed a hand down his face, looking as if he wasn't sure whether to puke or pass out.

He lifted his focus to her. "You want to know the real reason Isabel died that night?"

She clenched her jaw. "Daniel. It wasn't your fault. You couldn't have known—"

"That's not why. I know I wasn't the one to kill her, but damn it, Arrynn…it's still my fault."

"It's not—"

"I waited, okay? Longer than usual. I saw her disappear onto that trail, and I just stood there, staring at the emptiness. Because I knew. I knew that, despite what I told myself, despite the flowers and the wine, I was already gone. That whatever she gave me would be nothing more than a temporary fix. Another fucking bandaid we'd put over a gaping wound that would continue to bleed until there was nothing left inside either of us but hate. That whatever love we might have felt had long since withered and died."

He shook his head, kicking at the floor. "Tell me— when have you ever witnessed the resurrection of something and had it be a good thing? Had it come close to being true?" He snorted. "I'll tell you—never. Once something dies, it's only a shell that returns."

Arrynn swallowed past the lump in her throat, holding back tears as she crossed over to him. She took one hand, pressing it against her chest as she made eye contact. "I know you think that makes what happened your fault—"

"It does."

"No, sweetie, it doesn't. Because she *should* have been safe. *Should* have been waiting for you at that pond. A monster took her from you. And, if it hadn't been that day, that place... Look me in the eyes, and tell me Jacob wouldn't have tried, again? Wouldn't have found another way to get to her. He was your best friend, Daniel. You trusted him. He would have gotten to her, eventually. That's why this haunts you. Because you know there was nothing you could have done differently to stop it."

His shoulders drooped in seeming defeat. "I could have confronted him."

"Did you ever think he was capable of killing her?"

A strangled groan rumbled through his chest. "No."

"You've dedicated your life to putting monsters to rest. Don't you think it's time you let this one go? Forgive yourself as easily as you do everyone else?"

"You say it like it's easy."

"Not easy. Just necessary." She gave him an encouraging smile. "I'll make you a deal. You reheat our coffee, and I'll cook us breakfast. Might even have time to seduce you into another round before we head into the office."

He arched a brow. "Are you trying to distract me with the promise of food and sex?"

"Pretty much."

He grinned, the familiar sparkle back in his eyes. "You're on. Dry off while I go nuke the coffee. Just be warned. The next session isn't going to be quick, so I suggest you eat up when you get the chance."

Heat blossomed in her stomach, coiling tight, again. She watched him move toward the bed before turning. She took care of a few basic necessities then stared in the mirror as she washed her hands. Steam still obscured most of the surface, water streaking down the length. She smiled at the thought of spending an hour or two with Daniel outside of the damn office—allowing herself that simple pleasure before immersing herself back in Jimmy's case.

Guilt reared, but she tamped it down. After waiting for what felt like forever, surely she and Daniel deserved a few hours of uncomplicated happiness.

Mine.

The voice resonated through her head, the eerie rasp prickling the hairs on her nape. She looked up, pinned by the woman staring back at her in the mirror, white dress tattered and blood smattered—eyes a bloody shade of red.

Arrynn spun, nothing but an empty room greeting her. She searched the area, uneasiness prickling her skin as she moved over to the doorway, peering out. Everything looked the same as it had when Daniel had carried her in, other than a set of handcuffs conspicuously positioned on the center of his bed.

Desire shot through her stomach, making her skin tingle in anticipation, and she wondered how he'd react when she suggested she be the one to use them on him. Some of the tension eased at the thought. Obviously, the stress and fatigue were playing tricks on her mind. Between losing Jimmy and talking about Isabel with Daniel, it wasn't surprising Arrynn was imagining the woman's ghost, too. Hell, she considered it a godsend it wasn't Jimmy's spirit, as well.

What she and Daniel needed was a vacation—warm water and endless beaches. Bottomless margaritas with tiny umbrellas. Nothing but skin and lips and love. She made a mental note to talk to Daniel about heading south as she turned back, gasping when a woman appeared only inches away, her body no longer see-through. Arrynn's breath misted around them, a deep chill searing her skin.

The apparition sneered at her, exposing a flash of white teeth amidst thin, pale lips. "He'll never be yours, bitch. I'll see to that."

CHAPTER EIGHT

Daniel grabbed the mugs out of the microwave, checking the temperature before heading back toward the bedroom, noting the way his hands shook ever so slightly as uncertainty clawed at him. He hadn't planned on talking about Isabel. About that night, but damn it, Arrynn had a way of getting under his skin. Of making him face what he'd rather leave buried, festering until it infected everything he did. Touched. And he didn't know whether that made him love her more or want to strangle her.

The thought had him missing a step, and he cursed as a few drops scalded the back of his hand. God, the last thing he needed now was to blurt out that he'd fallen in love with her. Not after seeing her expression earlier. As if she wasn't sure whether to stay or bolt out the door. He knew allowing work to come between them hadn't been a wise choice, but becoming lovers had shaken him harder then he'd anticipated. And he hadn't pressed for more.

He paused outside his doorway. He'd already let his job ruin one relationship. Taint it beyond repair. He'd be damned before he made that same mistake, again. Not with Arrynn. Not when he'd come to the daunting realization that she might actually be the woman he wanted to spend his life with. That what they'd felt had been far more than merely an outlet for their grief over losing Jimmy. That his feelings for her were real. Raw. Unrelenting. As if he was hungry for something he'd never quite get his fill of. This was what had been lacking between him and Isabel. Why he'd known that day in the woods that, despite the effort, it would never be enough. *He'd* never be enough.

He hung his head as he gathered his control. He needed to get his mind in the game. He'd left his handcuffs on the bed in response to Arrynn's comment about indulging in another round of fun before allowing reality to intrude. Going in there hyperventilating over the fact he'd fallen in love with her wasn't really going to set the mood. And, in case she didn't return his feelings, he didn't want to lose another chance to hold her. Feel her come all over his mouth or cock. Hear her whisper his name as if he held far more than just her body.

He plastered on a smile as he walked through the door. "Arrynn? Sweetheart, I'd hoped your ass would be on the bed by now—those cuffs dangling from one pretty little wrist... Shit!"

He dropped the mugs as Arrynn flew backwards into the room, tumbling across the floor before landing in a heap at the side of the bed. Crimson lines marred her neck, the blood just starting to drip. He managed a step forward before Isabel appeared in front of him, fisting his shirt then flinging him into the far wall. His head hit hard, sparking dots across his vision.

He blinked, rolling onto his hands and knees, only to be picked up and shoved against the wall. Angry eyes stared back at him, her skin a deathly shade of white.

Isabel snarled at him, tossing him, again, screaming before she teleported to the other side of the room, grabbing hold of him. She shook him, his feet dangling above the floor. "You belong to me!"

He stilled as an invisible force closed around his throat, cutting off his airway. He clawed at his neck, only feeling his skin beneath his fingers, when white powder exploded below her, spraying like dust into the air. Isabel shrieked, her form whirling into a cloud before dissipating in a swirl of gray. Daniel fell to his knees, palming his chest as he fought to draw enough air to stop from passing out.

Small hands clasped his arm, then moved to cup his chin. "Damn it, Daniel, are you okay? Can you breathe?"

He nodded, blinking a few more times before giving Arrynn a hint of a smile. "Fine." He coughed, his throat feeling as if he'd swallowed glass.

"You're not fine, you jackass. Christ, you've got burns all over your skin."

"Says the woman with claw marks on her neck." He brushed his thumb next to the scratches. "Damn it, Arrynn. They're deep. You need… No."

He cursed as Arrynn's body slammed into the floor then jerked backwards, sliding along the wood before crashing into the wall beside the bed.

Daniel pushed to his feet, his gaze never leaving the spirit floating several feet away. "Enough, Isabel!"

The apparition spun to face him, flickering in and out

before appearing mere inches from his face, making his breath mist around them. "You wanted me gone."

"Not like this. Never like this."

"You never loved me!"

He calmed his voice. "Hurting Arrynn won't bring you back. Nothing you do will change what happened. You need to cross over—find peace."

Her body twitched at his words, her form flickering, again. She glanced over her shoulder as Arrynn managed to gain her feet, hissing then rising up toward the ceiling before vanishing. Daniel leaned against the wall as Arrynn limped over to him, moving in beside him.

She released a painful sigh. "Guess it wasn't all in your head, huh?"

He chuckled. "Guess not."

"Makes me wonder why she waited until now to attack. Lord knows she could have picked a far less convenient time."

"You mean like in the shower?"

Arrynn gave him a playful swat. "Make fun all you want, but yeah...I'd have thought us making love would have been more of a trigger for her than me alone in your bathroom."

His traitorous heart skipped at her choice of words, some of the rawness still tensing his muscles soothed by the mere fact she hadn't referred to them as simply "fucking".

"Probably for the same reason she left, now. She's weak." He held up his hand when Arrynn gawked at him. "I know. It sure as shit didn't feel weak, but she's done far worse. Makes me wonder where she's been and what she's been using her energy for."

Arrynn frowned. "You think she's haunting someone else?"

"It would explain why she disappears for days or even weeks at a time. Takes a lot of power to physically interact with people and things."

"I can only think of one other person she'd go after."

Daniel nodded, a dull ringing sound pounding inside his head at the thought. "Jacob. Can't say that I'm all that bothered by the idea of her tossing his ass around his jail cell."

"Me, either. Though it does raise the irritating question of how she's managing to manifest, at all, not to mention in more than one place." She pushed off the wall, turning to face him. "I'm sorry I didn't put much stock in this before."

"No apologies required. I thought I was crazy, too."

"I never thought..." She grinned. "Okay, maybe a bit, but now that we know you're not, we need to figure out what her connection is to our side of the veil."

"We will, but not until after we wrap up Jimmy's case." He held up his hand, again. "It's going to take her a while to recharge. In the meantime, we'll take precautions. Then, when we've dealt with what killed Jimmy, we'll concentrate on putting Isabel to rest—for good, this time."

She looked as if she was gong to argue then nodded, releasing an exasperated breath. "Fine."

He brushed his finger along her collarbone, next to the wounds. "I should clean those. Bandage them."

"You don't look any better." She waved him off. "I'm fine. They've already stopped bleeding."

"Stubborn." He glanced at the bed. "Thinking our *playtime* is on hold, for now."

She sighed but nodded.

"Right." Daniel straightened. "Then, it's clothes and back to work."

"I'll call Tanner. See if Barry was able to work his magic, yet, and get us Jimmy's things."

Daniel grabbed the rest of his clothes, quickly dressing before gathering up the broken bits of mug and tossing them in the garbage. He glanced at Arrynn. She'd already pulled on her pants and shirt and seemed busy tying her hair in a ponytail. He sighed. He'd been looking forward to losing himself in her, again. Feeling that silky hair wrapped around his fingers as he fisted it, holding her head in place as he claimed her body. Felt her surrender to him, again.

Arrynn's easy laughter jerked him from his thoughts as she closed the distance between them before drawing her finger along his chest. "Something tells me that work is the last thing on your mind."

He caught her hand, holding it over his heart as he layered his on top. "Not true. It's just that you're the first. But then, it's been that way for a long time, so...I'm used to it."

Her eyes widened in surprise before she gave him a guarded smile. Fuck, he must have hit his head far harder than he'd thought to be letting sappy shit like that just blurt out. And after telling himself now wasn't the time for declarations of undying love.

He cleared his throat, waving at the door. "After you."

Arrynn nodded, retrieving her phone as she headed for the front door. He followed her, listening to her talk to

Tanner. He checked behind them. Despite what he'd told Arrynn, he couldn't quite shake the feeling they were being watched. That Isabel wasn't as gone as he hoped.

Arrynn handed him her keys as they headed outside, mouthing for him to drive as she continued her conversation with Tanner. Daniel slipped behind the wheel, belted up, then started the car. The steady hum of the engine calmed his nerves as he left his house in the rearview and headed toward town.

Arrynn palmed his arm. "Tanner left the precinct about twenty minutes ago. They released the physical evidence, so he thought he'd pick it up on his way home. Something about him and Garret working around the clock for the past few days. He said we could meet him there. He and Garret would like to have a peek at it with us before we take it back to the center, if you're all right with that."

Daniel scoffed. "Tanner wants to look at our evidence? Please tell me they aren't thinking about switching divisions. They're not quite as bad as I'd thought, but having to work with them on a daily basis…" He feigned a shiver.

Arrynn laughed. "Hell no. I think they just feel bad that they've been riding your ass all this time, only to discover that ghosts are pretty damn badass. I actually think it's kind of sweet that they want to help."

"Lord knows we can use it. All those hours scouring files, and we're no closer to figuring out what happened. How a vengeful spirit just popped up and killed Jimmy. Speaking of which…what's happening to his body?"

Arrynn sighed. "The director is arranging for it to be brought to the center. He'll want us to take care of it once we've closed Jimmy's case. Ensure he stays peacefully on the other side."

"I owe the man that much."

"We both do, Daniel. This isn't on you."

He nodded, wishing he could believe that. "As long as we make it right, which would be easier to do if we could get some quality sleep. I hope Tanner and Garret have some decent coffee. I need the caffeine fix."

"Pretty sure they live on the stuff."

He glanced at her neck, hating the raised welts that seemed to openly mock him. While Arrynn was more than capable of handling herself, he couldn't help but feel as if he'd somehow failed her.

Arrynn swatted him. "Stop."

"Stop what?"

"Staring at me like this is all your fault. It's not."

He pursed his lips, turning at the next traffic light. "Isabel only attacked you because you were with me."

"We're partners, Daniel." She choked back a chuckle. "Hell, we're far more than that. Which means I won't be leaving your side anytime soon." She skimmed her fingers over the marks. "These are just a reminder to be more vigilant."

"Are you going to insist on winning every discussion we have?"

Her smile dropped his stomach. "Oh, sweetie, I already do."

He shook his head, smiling to himself. The girl definitely had a way about her. An easy silence stretched between them as he wove through some obscure streets, finally arriving at the address Arrynn had given him.

He stared at what looked like an industrial building. "You sure they live here?"

Arrynn shrugged, opening the door. "They share a loft apartment. Something about being up high. Access points. Damned if I know. What we hunt moves through walls, so...none of that shit's going to save us."

Daniel followed her to the main entrance, jumping when it unlocked just as they stopped. "Christ. Am I the only one creeped out by the fact they're watching us?"

She laughed, shaking her head as she opened the door, following the hallway down to an old elevator. "I'd be more concerned this thing's going to fall than whether or not Garret and Tanner are spying on us."

"Still don't like confined spaces, I see."

She stuck her tongue out at him, pressing the button for the top floor. She grabbed his arm as the unit jerked into motion, her fingers digging in slightly. He sighed, gathering her in his arms, enjoying the few precious moments of having her snugged against him. She leaned against him, dropping a quick kiss on his jaw before easing free as the elevator rattled to a halt.

Daniel released her, wishing it didn't feel as if it was the last time he'd get to hold a part of her. That she hadn't somehow slipped away without him realizing it. He sighed inwardly at the thought, mustering a smile as the doors opened. Tanner and Garret looked up from behind a large table.

Tanner waved them inside. "Thought you two might appreciate being somewhere different. Not have to stare at the same set of walls..." He pointed at Arrynn's neck. "What the hell happened to you?"

Arrynn sighed but stayed oddly silent.

Tanner frowned, nodding at Daniel. "Don't suppose you want to explain?"

Daniel crossed his arms over his chest. "Isabel's back."

Garret stepped around to their side, checking out Arrynn's wounds then tipping Daniel's head to get a better look at the marks. "A ghost did this to both of you? Damn. Any idea what set her off?"

"You mean besides being dead?" Daniel snorted. "Thinking she's not happy I'm still alive."

Garret opened his mouth then closed it, taking what appeared to be a calming breath. "Tanner and I aren't the enemy, here. I know we've had our fair share of differences, but...you guys are still part of the team. Family, I guess. As we see it, only Tanner and I are allowed to give you jerks a hard time. I didn't mean the question to be antagonistic. Ghosts just aren't our specialty. So, humor us, and answer the question. Why now? She's been dead for three years. And how? I thought you dispatched her ass just after you joined?"

Daniel took a step back. Fuck, when the hell had the two men become human? He glanced at Arrynn, but she merely nodded, batting at Tanner as the man dabbed something against her neck.

Tanner tsked her. "I'm immune to those puppy-dog looks you give Daniel, so stop fighting me. You know this is getting cleaned. Make peace with it." He glanced at Daniel. "You'll be next, but until then...help us out."

Daniel released a weary breath, leaning his hip on the table behind them. "Fine. Yes. I salted and burnt everything I could think of that was associated with Isabel shortly after joining up. Her bones, her clothes, her jewelry. And it seemed to work, until about a year ago—"

"A year ago?" Garret shook his head. "You've been seeing her fucking ghost for a year and didn't say anything?"

"I thought it was all in my head, jackass. And the last thing I needed was to have everyone here thinking I'd lost it. Besides, it was nothing. A voice, then her body misting in and out, the odd time. I figured it was fatigue or guilt." He scrubbed a hand down his face. "Apparently, I was wrong, unless Arrynn's having the same delusional dream —one that tosses people across the damn room and nearly chokes them to death."

Garret glanced at Tanner, releasing a weary sigh. He walked to the table, grabbing something off the top before returning to Daniel's side and holding a cell out to him. Daniel looked down, staring at the phone, not quite sure what Garret's point was, when the man activated the screen. A ghostly image stared back at him, the semi-transparent torso fading into nothing. But it was the familiar curve of the apparition's jaw that stole Daniel's breath.

Garret met his gaze. "Make that three of you. Jimmy was seeing a ghost, too. In fact, we're pretty sure he was dating one."

CHAPTER NINE

"He was what?" Arrynn batted at Tanner's hand, again. "Damn it, Tanner, it's a fucking scratch. I'll live. So, forget it, and get back to the part where Garret said Jimmy was dating a ghost."

Tanner stepped back, sighing when Garret motioned for him to do the talking. "You two might want to sit down."

Arrynn moved woodenly over to the chair Daniel pulled out for her, collapsing on it when her legs gave out. She wasn't sure if it was the sudden drop in adrenaline or just her emotions finally catching up with her. Either way, she wasn't looking forward to what Tanner and Garret had to say.

Daniel placed a comforting hand on her shoulder, leaning down to her, his lips dangerously close to her. "You okay? I can grab us some coffee, food, if you need some time before talking about this." He sighed. "Should have stopped on the way over here after our plans got railroaded."

"We can get something on the way back to the center. I'd just really like to know what the hell's going on."

Daniel nodded, brushing his thumb along her neck before focusing on the other men. Arrynn drew a deep breath, glancing at Tanner and Garret.

She arched a brow at their smug grins. "What?"

Tanner chuckled as he turned to Garret. "Pay up, buddy. I win."

Garret shoved his hand in his pocket, handing over twenty bucks before shaking his head at them. "After two years of eye fucking each other, you two couldn't wait until after you'd closed this case to finally get it on? I'm disappointed, guys."

Arrynn's mouth hinged open, but nothing came out save for a small raspy breath.

Tanner laughed, again. "Please. We're hunters. And we'd be pretty shitty ones if we couldn't read the sexual tension between you two since pretty-boy here walked through the door. Then, after what happened to Jimmy... all that pent-up stress." He shrugged. "Seemed reasonable you two might seek some form of mutual release."

Garret punched his buddy in the shoulder. "What Tanner means is...it's about time. You both deserve a bit of happiness. We're happy for you...even if it did cost me twenty bucks. Not to mention the fact the jackass will be impossible to live with, now, but..." He waved at the table of evidence. "Shall we get back to work?"

He didn't wait for an answer, motioning to the phone. "That's from the night Jimmy was attacked. He must have taken a picture just before it happened. Thankfully, Barry convinced his colleagues that Jimmy played with graphic images as a hobby. Wasn't a hard sell, if you know what I mean? People don't like to consider explanations that involve ghosts or werewolves."

Arrynn looked at the image as Daniel handed her the phone. Her breath caught, her gaze whipping to his. She reached for his hand, threading her fingers through his. "I'm so sorry, Daniel."

Garret closed in on them. "For what?"

She didn't miss the way Daniel drew himself up, once again shielding himself with the walls she'd tried to break down. She waited for him to pull his hand away, her heart kicking up when he simply stood there, their fingers still entwined.

She looked at Tanner then Garret. "That's not just any ghost. That's Isabel."

Garret's mouth pinched tight as he glanced at Daniel then back to her. "You sure?"

Daniel huffed. "Of course, she's sure. We just went a few rounds with Isabel's pissed-off spirit at my house. Trust me. It's her." He motioned to the phone. "But what makes you think he was dating her?"

Garret touched the screen, activating one of the applications. "There're a bunch of messages on his phone. They sounded like static until we filtered it out. This is what was hiding underneath."

"You belong to me, James."

Garret stopped the recording. "I might not hunt ghosts, but I know the difference between a human voice and one that's not. And that isn't fucking human."

Arrynn nodded. "Not anymore. It's called an EVP. An electronic voice phenomenon. Basically, it's a ghost communicating through the white noise on the phone."

"It's creepy as hell, is what it is."

"But how did you know to dig deeper? I'm assuming the cops didn't or the case would still be open."

"All the evidence pointed to an animal attack. And the phone was damaged. Thankfully, Tanner has some wicked computer skills. But I'm assuming the police thought the messages had been compromised and erased." Garret shrugged. "As for digging deeper...werewolf alphas are able to communicate at a frequency we can't hear without a special filter. Took a chance these weren't simply a series of blank messages." Garret played another. "But that's not what a werewolf alpha sounds like, which pointed to your theory about a ghost. Some of the recordings go on like that for a minute straight. Which, based on the content, means Jimmy thought she was real. That they were a couple. How is that even possible?"

Arrynn stood, pacing across the room before spinning and leaning on the far wall. "Ghosts have far greater powers than merely popping in and out of places. They can manipulate temperature, move objects...inflict wounds. They're super strong, super fast, not to mention incredibly hard to get rid of. They've been known to possess people, mimic voices and, in some cases, manipulate reality. Isabel is strong. Not impossible that Jimmy never suspected what she really was before it was too late, and he was already under her spell."

Garret huffed. "Give me a damn werewolf any day over this bullshit."

Arrynn looked at Daniel. "I'm starting to think your hunch that you'd been set up that night was right. That maybe Isabel sent you that message to ensure you didn't inadvertently show up and try to stop her."

Daniel's fists clenched at his side. "So, why didn't she contact you?"

"Maybe she knew I was headed home. Had taken the night off."

"Seems odd."

"She's a ghost, Daniel. One filled with pain and rage and hate. Trust me, she's not thinking clearly. Her actions are purely instinct driven. She was killed by a man. Seems reasonable she'd lash out at them, first."

The muscle in his jaw tensed. "She did this because of me."

"Fuck that." Arrynn walked over to him. "She did this because of Jacob. Because she was murdered. Because she refuses to cross over. This isn't on you."

Tanner stepped into view beside her. "Thinking we should worry more about how we're going to stop this, than about placing blame. Though, for the record, Danno, Arrynn's right. This is way beyond fucked up and definitely not anything any of us could have guessed at." He nudged her. "Garret and I might not be highly knowledgeable when it comes to ghosts, but even we know they're usually bound, right? To where they died, or a house."

"They are." Arrynn scrubbed a hand down her face. "Which means there's still something on our side of the veil giving her access. Something we missed."

"Gotta be a few somethings if she's moving around." Daniel raked a hand through his hair, looking as if he wanted to pull some of it out. "That's the part I don't get. It's not just my place—it's at the center, Jimmy's. What the hell could possibly connect them?"

Tanner glanced at Garret, something unspoken passing between them.

Arrynn groaned. "Just spit it out, Tanner."

He clenched his jaw. "Could it be you, Cartwright? Personally?"

Daniel's expression hardened, as the muscle in his temple flexed. "It's possible—"

"No!" Arrynn gave him a tap on the shoulder. "That's not how it works. You know that."

"Just because we've never come across that kind of haunting—"

"No. Ghosts are bound by what belonged to them. Despite what Isabel believes, hell what lots of messed up folks think, people don't belong to other people. It's not you."

Tanner cleared his throat, gaining their attention. "So, the answer should be in with the evidence or still at Jimmy's, right?"

Arrynn sighed. "Theoretically."

"Then, let's focus on the shit we have some control over." Tanner grinned. "Figure four sets of eyes are better than two. We didn't get a chance to look at anything other than the phone before you two showed up."

Daniel took a step toward Tanner. "You guys don't have to—"

"Just shut up and start going through those pictures. There's a ton of them. Garret will look through with you. Arrynn can scan through the reports with me. That way, we shouldn't miss anything."

Daniel gave Tanner a half smile. "Thanks."

"Like Garret said. Jimmy was family. A crazy-ass cousin-type, but family nonetheless."

"And that's the Tanner I know." Daniel shuffled over. "Fine, Garret can help me…"

A blare of music drowned out the rest of his words. Daniel muttered something under his breath, pulling his cell from his pocket. He touched the surface then put the unit to his ear.

"Cartwright."

His brow drew together as he listened to someone on the other end, the voice nothing more than a murmur of noise.

He frowned. "Warden Sinclair. Yes, I'm that Daniel Cartwright. How can I help you?" His breath caught, and he glanced at Arrynn, the color draining from his face. "Are you sure?" He nodded, jaw muscle jumping, again. "No, I appreciate the call. I'll head over."

He lowered the phone, staring off into nothing. Arrynn moved over to him, waiting for him to acknowledge her. When he simply stood there, still staring into space, she placed her hand on his chest. His heart thrashed against her palm, the erratic rhythm spiking a wave of fear.

She drew a deep breath. "Daniel?"

He blinked, tipping his head down to look at her. "Yeah?"

"What's wrong?"

He seemed genuinely puzzled by her question. "What?"

"The phone call. You mentioned Warden Sinclair. What did he want?"

His face got impossibly whiter as he swung his gaze to Tanner, Garret, then back to her. "He was calling about Jacob."

"Jacob? As in Jacob Bowell. *The* Jacob?"

"Yeah. Seems there was an incident at the prison. Sinclair wanted to inform me that Jacob's dead."

"He's what?"

Daniel recognized Arrynn's voice, but he couldn't manage to add anything over the dull roar sounding in his head. Jacob was dead. After wishing for that very outcome for years, having it suddenly become reality shifted something inside his gut, making him thankful he hadn't taken the time to eat anything. Mixed emotions battled for dominance, nothing but a numbing cold winning out.

Arrynn's hand traced a path along his jaw, drawing his attention back to her. "You okay?"

"I..." He carded a hand through his hair. "Honestly, I don't know."

She motioned to one of the chairs. "Thinking you might want to sit before you faceplant on the floor."

He moved with her, taking the seat without really acknowledging it. A volley of memories played in his head, flashing in sequence like an old movie reel. He wasn't sure how long he'd sat there when a large hand landed on his shoulder. He shook away the thoughts, focusing on Tanner.

The man held out a glass with some brown liquid. "Here. Drink this."

He took the glass, sniffing it. The heady alcohol aroma had him turning his head. "Dear god, what is this?"

"Just drink the damn thing, Cartwright."

Daniel scowled but knocked back the shot, eyes widening as the whiskey burned a path through his chest.

He coughed, eyeing Tanner. "Where the hell did you get that? It's like gasoline."

Tanner grinned. "Garret and I brew our own. Have a homemade still in the back room. That stuff's one-hundred and twenty proof."

"That stuff just burnt a hole in my gut." He thanked Garret when the man offered him some juice. "You do realize I have to stay sober, right?"

"Please. That wasn't more than a sip. You'll be fine, just...let Arrynn drive." Tanner winked at him. "To be safe."

Daniel leaned back in the chair. He still couldn't believe Jacob was dead. While a part of him hated the man Jacob had become, another still remembered all the years they'd been friends. The boy Daniel had grown up with.

Arrynn knelt in front of him, gently taking a hand in his. "I'm sorry."

Daniel shook his head. "The man was a monster. He deserved whatever he got."

"Daniel. He was your best friend for over twenty years. You just don't forget all that time overnight."

"No, you don't. But I've had three years to get used to the idea that I would have been better off never having met him."

She merely nodded. "So, why did you tell Sinclair you'd head over?"

A roil of nausea churned through his gut. Christ, he shouldn't feel at all sorry for the man. Not after what he'd become. "Apparently, Jacob named me as his next of kin. They want me to pick up his personal effects."

"You?" She glanced at the other two men, her expression clearly suggesting she thought she'd heard him wrong. "Why would he do that? I mean, when's the last time you saw the man?"

Daniel steeled away his emotions. "The day they locked his ass up for life." He stood. "We should go." He turned to Tanner, but the man waved him off.

"You and Arrynn go. Garret and I will root through this stuff. You can come back once you're done. We'll call you if we find anything obvious. Just…take care of business. Fairly certain your ghost isn't going anywhere. A few hours won't change that."

He nodded, heading for the stairs. He wasn't sure what they'd find at the prison, but his instincts told him nothing good would come of it.

CHAPTER TEN

Daniel sat in the passenger seat as Arrynn pulled out of the prison parking lot, sun setting low, a brown cardboard box on his lap. The warden had met with them in his office, that same box positioned on the corner of his desk. He hadn't elaborated on the details surrounding Jacob's death, just that Jacob had been found slashed in the showers by one of the guards.

The man had sworn he'd keep them informed on the progress of their investigation, though it had felt more like a token vow than an actual promise. The entire exchange had taken less than thirty minutes, ending with Daniel signing for Jacob's personal effects. Now, they were heading south with no particular destination in mind.

He stared at the lid, uncertain whether he wanted to open it or simply burn it, sight unseen. A testament to his new life. Of finally letting go of the past.

"You know that box isn't going to open itself, Daniel."

He grinned at the teasing tone in Arrynn's voice. She'd

been a rock. Deftly answering any questions regarding their employment without actually saying anything. The woman could be a damn politician.

He looked over at her, admiring the way the setting sun highlighted the gold streaks in her hair. She was more than stunning. "Haven't decided if I want to look inside, yet." He chuckled at the way the skin over her nose crinkled. "I know. Pretending it doesn't exist isn't an option. Doesn't mean I have to like it."

"I was thinking we'd head back to Tanner and Garret's place. Open it there. Betting Tanner would give you another shot of that whiskey."

"Are you trying to get me drunk so you can seduce me? Because all it would take is you pulling the car over to the side of the road."

Her easy laughter surrounded them. "Wouldn't that be great? The two of us getting arrested for indecent exposure. Bet the director would love that."

He swept his gaze along the length of her. "Thinking you'd be worth any form of punishment, sweetheart."

Her eyes gleamed at his words. "I'll keep that in mind." She turned onto a deserted two lane. "The GPS says this will cut our time in half. As long as we don't break down, because I'm not sure anyone uses this road."

"So, pulling over is definitely back on the table."

The corners of her mouth hitched up. "How about I pull over and you can drive so I can give you the best damn blowjob of your life without slowing us down?"

Daniel's cock jumped inside his pants as the image of her sucking him off as he drove flashed in his head. He placed his hand on her leg, smoothing his fingers along her inner thigh—just brushing the backs of his knuckles against her pussy. "Or I could shove your pants down and wedge my head between your legs."

A breathy rasp escaped her lips, and she squirmed in her seat, her breathing noticeably rougher. "Do you want us to crash? Because there's no way I'd be able to keep this vehicle on the road if you touch my clit. I'm still on edge from this morning."

"As I recall, you came more than once this morning."

"True. But I had plans of using those handcuffs you just happened to leave on the bed."

"Oh, sweetheart. While I love your enthusiasm, only one of us was getting cuffed to the bed."

"Of course. You."

He grinned. "Damn, I love your sense of humor."

She tensed at his choice of words before visibly relaxing. She glanced at the box. "Not to be a buzzkill, but did it seem odd to you that Sinclair didn't want to discuss how Jacob died?"

Daniel shrugged. "There's an ongoing investigation. That's fairly standard. Though, I'll admit, he seemed… twitchy. And overly interested in exactly what our department investigated, regardless of how many times you insisted we were only there because Jacob had named me as his next of kin."

"Call me paranoid, but I'm starting to wonder if Jacob was killed by something…supernatural."

"Hell of a coincidence that Jacob ends up dead the same week as Jimmy. And just when Isabel makes her grand reappearance. Her killing him would explain why she didn't bother me for a week—between the two attacks, she was too drained. It would also explain why she'd disappeared previously. She was tormenting Jacob."

"Can't say I blame her for wanting revenge. I'm just glad Jacob's being cremated, later today. The last thing we need is him popping up as another vengeful spirit."

"Amen to that. But I still don't understand how she got to him. I mean...I work with Jimmy. It's possible I left something at his house that gave Isabel access, but Jacob? I haven't set foot inside that prison before today. How the hell was she able to materialize there?"

Arrynn motioned to the box. "Maybe the answer's sitting on your lap."

"Guess we'll find— *Look out!*"

Daniel grabbed the handle above his head as Isabel's ghostly form appeared in front of them, filling the windshield with an eerie white mist. Arrynn swerved, driving off the road and onto the dirt shoulder. Dust and gravel kicked up into the air as the car rocked to a halt.

Daniel reached for Arrynn. "You okay?"

She nodded, coughing as some of the dust billowed into the car through the vents. "Damn it. I should have just rammed through her, but..."

"But it was creepy as fuck. Yeah, I get it." He grabbed the box off the floor where it'd fallen during the skid. "But I think we have our answer. There's got to be something inside here that's allowing her to materialize."

"Thinking we should—"

Arrynn's voice cut off as her door flew open, followed by the click of her seatbelt. Daniel grabbed her arm, but she slipped through his grasp as she was flung out of the car, rolling across the dirt. Daniel popped the trunk release then grabbed the box, quickly stepping out of the car. He headed toward the back, only to fall face first onto the ground as hands wrapped around one ankle. He cursed as the force pulled his leg under the car, dragging him across the gravel. Stones bit into his hands as he tried to stop the movement, finally wedging his other foot on the frame.

He curled his fingers around the open door, using it and his leg to counter Isabel's pressure, unsure how to break her hold, when footsteps crunched beside him. He looked to his left as Arrynn stopped, shotgun in hand. She bent low and aimed the barrel under the car, shooting a round of salt next to his leg. A high-pitched screech filled the air then the hold vanished. He fell backwards, groaning as more rocks poked his back.

Arrynn loomed over him, dirt smeared across her face —the dusty residue caked with blood on one temple. She offered him her hand, helping him to his feet before moving to the trunk. She reappeared, a moment later, salt in one hand, a tire iron cradled under her other arm. He took the iron as she cocked the shotgun, both of them scouring the surrounding area.

Arrynn wiped her mouth with the back of her hand. "I think she's gone."

"The question is, for how long?"

She nodded at the box as Daniel knocked it toward them. "We could just torch the fucker. To be sure."

"Hell yeah. But, if we don't know what's drawing her, we might not recognize a link to Jimmy's stuff. We need to take a look inside, first."

"A circle of salt won't stop her with that box inside

with us. She'll be able to materialize within the boundaries."

He sighed as he broke through the tape on the top. "I know."

He tore one flap as he opened the lid, dumping the contents onto the ground. Arrynn shifted on her feet, still searching the immediate area, as Daniel quickly sorted through the contents.

"Nothing here looks like a possible link, unless there's something inside one of these letters."

"Search them...shit."

She hit the side of the vehicle, her body bending backwards over the trunk as Isabel appeared between them. Daniel swung at the apparition with his iron, grabbing hold of Arrynn when the ghost vanished, again.

He levered her up. "You all right?"

"I'm really starting to hate her. Just find her link so I can burn the fucker."

He went to his knees, shaking out the letters then rummaging through the contents. He'd just about given up hope when he spotted a tattered photograph. Green eyes looked back at him, the familiar sparkle stealing his breath. He stared at the woman—at them—until a firm shake drew him back. He blinked, focusing on Arrynn as she snapped her fingers in front of his face.

"Damn it, Daniel, we don't have time for you to zone out on me."

He opened his mouth then closed it, still staring at the photo.

Arrynn glanced over his shoulder, her sharp inhalation finally drawing him back. She nudged him. "That's a great photo, but isn't there something else? Pictures, alone, generally aren't enough to bind a soul to this side."

"I don't see anything else remotely connected to her." He flipped it over, again, frowning. "There's something tapped on the back."

He tugged at one corner, yanking off an old piece of thick paper. Faded words covered the opposite side, a reddish-brown smear down one edge.

"Is that a ticket stub? With her blood on it?"

"She was always cutting herself. She probably nicked her thumb trimming the edges of the photos. She had this thing about symmetry."

"I'm assuming it was an important event for her?"

"It was our last evening out before she was killed. We went to the theatre with Jacob. He'd bought the tickets as a gift. Had said he'd hoped it would be the start of a way back for us. They had someone taking photographs. She had two more copies printed. Gave one to each of us as a thank you." He looked up at her. "Do you think that's enough to bind her here?"

"A photo of her ex-lover and the man who killed her? At a turning point in her life? Coupled with a blood-smeared ticket? I'd say that could be a tangible link. Only one way to be sure, though."

"We burn them, and, poof, she can't manifest here."

Arrynn tossed him a lighter. "Let's burn, now, and talk about it later."

Daniel flicked the metal wheel, trying to get the damn thing to spark, when a set of hands shoved him backwards. He fell onto his ass, the impact knocking the lighter out of his hand. It bounced on the ground then slid under the car. "Fuck."

An explosion of salt filled the air, followed by Arrynn's hand on his collar. She reefed him onto his ass. "Get the lighter. I'll try to counter her strikes."

Daniel cursed under his breath. It was like a damn horror movie—dropping the only important weapon in a crucial moment. He went to his stomach, reaching under the vehicle. The cold plastic slid farther away as his fingers brushed the edge before he managed to get a grip on it. He dragged it toward him, only to have cold fingers encircle his wrist.

"She's got my arm."

Arrynn's face appeared next to his, just a few inches off the ground. She grabbed the tire iron from his other hand, swinging the metal under his wrist to sever Isabel's hold. He pulled free, a series of burns scarring his skin.

"Damn it, she hurt you."

Daniel waved it off, finally getting the device to light. "Just a reminder not to be so damn clumsy, next time."

He held the tiny flame under the corner of both the ticket and the photo until they hissed as fire spread across the surface, quickly turning the paper into a glowing pile of ash.

Arrynn darted around him, making a lopsided circle of salt on the ground before kneeling beside him. Her increased breath skated across his flesh. "Now, we wait."

He nodded, scanning their side of the road. The wind picked up, swirling a small dirt devil across the ground as the clouds bled from crimson into violet.

He glanced at her. "So far, so—"

He grunted as his body lifted off the ground, landing hard several feet away. Arrynn yelled his name, and he blinked the scenery into focus just as she tumbled across the gravel next to him. He stared as Isabel rose from within the circle, baring her teeth at them. She flowed forward only to stop as she hit the edge of the salt.

Daniel darted over to Arrynn, helping her onto her knees. "It must not have been the link."

"But it has to be…" Arrynn groaned. "Damn it, we're idiots. You said there were three copies of that picture."

"Yeah, so?"

"So, if she taped a bloody ticket to the back of each of them—"

He cursed inwardly. "We need to destroy all three."

"Where are the other two?"

"One's at my place, packed away in a box with more photos. The other's… Fuck, it's in my wallet."

He reached behind him, slipping the leather billfold out of his pocket. He thumbed to a section behind the bills, removing the ragged picture. "Shit! There's only half here."

"Just burn what you have. She's disappeared from within the circle, which means she'll be popping up around us, any second now."

He flicked the lighter, again, as Arrynn unloaded another buckshot of salt at Isabel, keeping her back. The edge of the picture caught then flared, smoke curling up from his hand. He dropped the flaming remains, watching as they turned to ash. Isabel shrieked, racing toward them, only to vanish as the last of the picture crumbled onto the ground, nothing more than gray dust. Daniel palmed the gravel, drawing in a few quick breaths before pushing to his feet.

Arrynn stumbled over to him, still staring at where Isabel had disappeared. "At least we know we're right about how she's manifesting. Those tickets and photos are like conduits to our side of the veil."

"Unfortunately, there're still one and a half pieces out there, fueling her." He scrubbed his face. "We need to call Garret and Tanner. If the other half of mine fell out at Jimmy's, giving her access—"

"It could be in with the evidence, which means they're at risk."

He pulled out his cell as they returned to the car, finding Tanner's contact information. Arrynn started the vehicle, turning onto the road as Daniel waited for Tanner to answer.

The man picked up on the fourth ring. "Christ, Cartwright, it hasn't been that long. We're still going through everything."

"Just, listen for a minute. We know Isabel's link. There's a photo of me, her and Jacob. It has a ticket taped on the back. We think half of mine fell out at Jimmy's place. Did you find anything like that?"

"There are like a hundred damn pictures in here. Barry had prints made up of everything they photographed."

"This one is ripped and weathered. It's important, Tanner. Isabel can manifest wherever that photo is."

"She can what? Shit! Garret, we need…"

Tanner's voice keened into a grunt as static blared through the earpiece, intermixed with shouts and sounds of fighting in the background.

"Tanner! Tanner! Shit!" He yanked the cell away from his ear. "Damn line just went dead."

The car shook slightly as Arrynn hit the accelerator. "I can get us there in ten minutes."

"Not sure they have that long."

"That's the best we can do." She balked at his scowl. "They're hunters. Granted, they deal with werewolves, but they're not helpless."

"I hope you're right, because after what we just did, there's no doubt in my mind Isabel's out for blood."

CHAPTER ELEVEN

"I swear ten minutes has never taken this damn long."

Arrynn looked over at Daniel, glancing at the way his fingers tapped restlessly on the dash. "Just another minute."

He met her gaze before staring out the window at the street as Arrynn whipped around a corner. "I swear, if she hurts them…"

"We have to trust they can hold their own. They *are* hunters, Daniel."

"*Were* hunters. Silver bullets and conventional weapons won't do shit to Isabel. And she's bound to be on the rampage. We both know it."

"They know about salt. I'm sure they're safe inside a circle, planning a suitable revenge."

Daniel chuckled. "Have I told you that I love your sense of humor? How you always manage to make any situation better?"

Arrynn grinned. "That better not be the only thing you love about me."

Daniel arched a brow, and she cursed under her breath. She hadn't meant for her comment to sound like a confession, but damn, it had. Hell, she might as well have tattooed, I love you, on her forehead. She ignored the way her heart rate kicked up at just thinking he could feel the same as she skidded the car to a halt, shoving it into first.

Daniel snagged her wrist before she could jump out. "For the record, it's not. Not even close." He brushed his thumb over her skin. "But thinking this isn't the time or place for *that* conversation. You armed?"

She licked her lips, wondering why her throat was suddenly so dry. "Um...yeah. Several more buck shots and a canister of salt. You?"

"Your lovely tire iron and salt I grabbed from the trunk." He motioned toward the loft. "As much as I want to dispatch Isabel, Garret and Tanner are our main concern. We can always torch her ass later."

"Agreed. Though, if I know Tanner, he won't leave until their place is 'theirs' again."

"The man is stubborn." He released her arm. "Let's go."

Arrynn jumped out of the car, jogging beside Daniel as they headed for the building. "I hope they left the damn door unlocked." She sighed when the handle turned in Daniel's hand. "Thank god."

They darted down the hallway, closing the gate on the old lift. The bell dinged as they reached the top floor, the iron gates creaking as they opened into Tanner and Garret's apartment. The main area was vacant, photographs and other papers scattered around the room.

Daniel flicked the light switch. The bulbs flashed on then off, returning the loft to nothing but shadows amidst the soft glow of the moon low on the horizon. He frowned. "At least, we got up here before she drained the power."

"That's because she wants us here."

Daniel arched a brow. "I said how I love that you make things better, not worse."

She shook her head, cautiously stepping forward. A blast of cold air preceded Isabel's first attack. The ghost appeared between them, sending them both flying across the room. Arrynn impacted the far wall, falling onto the floor as the world dimmed a bit.

Firm hands lifted her, shouldering most of her weight. "Fuck, sweetheart. Are you okay?"

Arrynn groaned, rubbing the back of her head as she gave Daniel a guarded nod. "How is she still able to toss us around? I'd have thought that between us and Garret and Tanner, she'd be drained."

"Anger and hatred are pretty damn powerful. Thinking the closer we get to sending her over, the more she feeds off of those emotions. But, if it's any consolation, this attack didn't hurt quite as much."

"Speak for yourself. Any sign of the guys?"

"Not, yet. But it's hard to see that much when you're soaring through the air. Betting they're holed up somewhere in the back of the apartment. At least, I hope they are."

Arrynn nodded, afraid her voice would betray her. Daniel already felt responsible for all the damage Isabel had done. She didn't need to add to that guilt by confirming his doubts.

Daniel sighed. "Any ideas how to hold her back long enough to find them and the photo?"

"Damned if I know. It's not like we can trap..." Her voice trailed off as she glanced toward the lift.

Daniel cursed under his breath. "Damn, you're amazing. It might just work."

Arrynn frowned. "But she'll need a reason to go in there."

"I'll give her one. Me."

"Daniel—"

"Not a debate, Arrynn." He silenced her with a finger over her lips. "Ultimately, this is about me. Blame or not, you know that's true. Which means I'm the logical choice, plain and simple. It has nothing to do with my faith in you. In fact, I'm trusting you to save my ass and slam the damn gates shut once she throws me across the room, again."

"And if she decides to shred you, instead?"

"I'm armed. I'll only allow her to think she's got the upper hand. Promise."

"We've always been armed. Hasn't stopped her from damn near killing us."

"She could have killed me a thousand times over in the past three years. She hasn't. I have to believe that's because she wants something more." He sighed, easing her away from him. "Just...be ready."

He took off, diving to one side when Isabel misted to form in front of him. He knocked over a chair, stumbling several steps before limping into the elevator, back to the far wall. Isabel billowed upwards, losing most of her cohesiveness as she floated toward him, stopping just shy of the doors.

Daniel grimaced as he shifted over. "What's wrong,

Isabel? Change your mind? Decided you don't want me to join you, after all?"

Her shape undulated then solidified. "You're mine."

"Then, come and show me the way."

She hesitated, glancing back at Arrynn before slowly creeping inside the lift. Daniel's hand fell to his side as he moved sideways. He didn't speak, just inched to his right as Isabel drew closer to him. She'd almost reached him when she seemed to hit an invisible barrier. Her gaze dropped to the floor and she hissed at the line of salt between them.

Daniel lunged toward the opening, trailing salt after him as he rolled through the doorway. Isabel screamed, racing forward, only to bounce back as Arrynn closed the gates. The ghost snarled, its anger clearly visible in the ugly twist of its features.

Arrynn helped Daniel up, huffing at the noticeable bruise coloring his forehead. "You're going to be a dozen shades of purple."

"As long as we're all still breathing, I doubt I'll care. I'll collect the evidence and put it in a garbage can. You go find Tanner and Garret, ensure they're okay and that they don't have the picture on them. Then, we'll torch the entire lot."

She glanced at Isabel. "How long do you think that will hold her?"

"Guess that depends on her energy level and how pure those bars are. I'm not holding my breath."

"Don't take any unnecessary risks while I'm gone or I swear I'll kick your ass."

"Oh, sweetheart, it's your ass that's going to get all the attention, just as soon as we're finished here. Now, go."

Arrynn grunted but took off, searching the kitchen then heading down a small hallway. The first two rooms were empty, though they'd clearly been ransacked by either the men or the ghost. Her stomach churned, her heart beating faster as she opened the final door. A shaft of moonlight illuminated the two men near the back of the room, huddled together on the floor—a circle of salt around them.

She darted forward, still wary of Isabel popping up, until she reached the boundary. Tanner looked up at her, squinting as if he couldn't quite focus on her.

His lips kicked up into a smile. "About bloody time. You two take the scenic route?"

She stepped inside the ring, kneeling beside them. "Isabel didn't like us showing up."

"Lady packs quite the punch." Tanner brushed back Arrynn's hair, exposing her cut. "You okay?"

"I think I should be asking you that." She let her head dip forward. "Christ, when your phone went dead on Daniel like that, we thought she'd—"

"Killed us?" Tanner snorted. "She certainly gave it her best try. Garret's going to be seeing stars for a week."

"As long as he's seeing something. Did you find that photograph? We've got her temporarily contained, but it won't hold her for long."

Tanner sighed as his shoulders drooped. "We tried, but she kept swirling everything all over the floor. Then, she'd toss us around like ragdolls whenever we tried to retrieve it. Nothing we threw at her seemed to have any effect until I swung one of Garret's cast iron pans at her." He grinned. "She didn't like that. But she got hold of Garret before he could get one. I've never seen someone hit a wall that hard. He's been in and out since. That's why I brought him back here. Don't think he can take another hit like that."

"Sounds like you did pretty well for a couple of wolf cops."

He simply stared at her.

She smiled. "Okay. Stay here. Daniel and I will burn everything we can find. Just needed to make sure you didn't have it."

He snagged her arm as she turned. "Fuck that. I can fight."

"Tanner..."

"Don't even think about lecturing me. We'll leave Garret here. He should be safe, right?" Tanner didn't even wait for her to nod. "We'll gather everything up and torch it. And, if she gets loose, she'll have three of us to deal with."

"Fine. Be stubborn. Just remember, salt and iron."

Tanner held up a large skillet. "Got a pan with her name on it."

Arrynn helped the other man up, ensuring the ring was still intact around Garret before making her way back to the entrance. She peeked down the hall, waving Tanner on. A dim light glowed at the end of the corridor, flicking shadows along the wall.

Arrynn rounded the corner, nearly running into Daniel. He dropped a bunch of papers and pictures into a garbage can he'd set alight, the hiss of the material catching fire resonating through the air. She glanced at the elevator. A white mist filled the space.

"I disconnected the fire alarms. Figured we didn't need anyone else showing up." Daniel released a weary breath.

"Guess I haven't found the damn picture, yet. She's still there." His jaw clenched. "I don't like this. She hasn't tried to escape. Makes me wonder if she's planning something."

"Doesn't matter. Once we burn that photo, she'll dissipate. It's got to be here somewhere. Tanner doesn't have it."

Daniel looked over her shoulder. "Looks like what he does have is a concussion. Where's Garret?"

Tanner grabbed some paper off the floor, tossing it into the can. "In the bedroom. He's a bit out of it."

"You don't look much better." Daniel clasped Tanner's arm when the man swayed on his feet. "Why don't you stay with Garret? Arrynn and I can finish this."

"Fuck that. If there's fighting to do, I'm in. I'll go check over by the sofas. There's bound to be stuff scattered everywhere."

Daniel muttered something under his breath. "He's right. There's shit all over the place. Might take longer than we have to find it."

Arrynn placed a hand on his arm. "We'll search for as long as we have. If she gets loose, we'll take the fire escape down. Regroup a bit before coming back. At least, we're pretty certain she's restricted to here and your place. That's a start."

Daniel grinned, planting a quick, hard kiss on her mouth. "See. Better. Go help Tanner. I'll search the opposite side."

"Don't do anything heroic, Daniel. She's not worth dying over."

"Nope. But you are. Now, go."

He took off, already searching under furniture. Arrynn

joined Tanner, gathering every piece of paper she could find.

Tanner grunted beside her. "Last fucking time I ask Barry to be so damn diligent. It's going to take more than a few minutes to find the rest of the pictures."

"Just pick up what you can. Maybe we'll get lucky."

Tanner chuckled. "Right, because things have really been going our way on this case."

"Jackass."

He pointed to an overturned chair. "I think I see more under there. Harder than hell to tell, though, with only the moonlight and Daniel's fire as light sources."

"I'll check."

She darted over, reaching under the chair until she grabbed hold of whatever Tanner had noticed. She pulled it out, staring down at Jimmy's torn body. Arrynn's stomach dropped. Even if they managed to torch the photo, there was still another one she and Daniel would have to deal with before this was truly over. Another chance for Isabel to win. To hurt someone else they cared about. Hell, to kill Daniel. Arrynn pushed aside the lingering doubts. Daniel wasn't an easy target and had more than proved he could handle Isabel.

She leaned over, again, sweeping her hand underneath the cushions, brushing across another ragged piece of paper. She rocked back on her heels, inhaling when Daniel's eyes gazed back at her.

She turned to Tanner. "Got it."

"Perfect. Then, let's torch it while she's still trapped."

Arrynn pushed upright, heading back toward the kitchen when a swirl of gray materialized directly in front of her, Isabel's form taking shape. Arrynn reacted, firing off a salt round at the spirit just as Tanner lunged forward, swinging the pan. Isabel hissed, shooting upwards and disappearing through the ceiling.

"Damn it. Arrynn. Tanner. Isabel's gone."

Tanner scoffed at Daniel. "No shit, Cartwright. We've got the—"

His voice cut off into a harsh grunt as his body flew backwards. He hit the toppled chair, rolling over it, a dull thud filling the air. Arrynn stopped as Isabel appeared in the hallway, eyes blazing red, half her body fading into nothing. The apparition hovered there, the air around them cooling. Arrynn cocked the shotgun, arching her brow in challenge.

"Enough!"

Daniel's voice boomed through the apartment. The ghost turned, hissing at Daniel as it loomed closer to him. Daniel stood his ground, holding her back with a wave of his tire iron. A salt bomb rested in his hand as he stared at the spirit.

"This has to stop, Isabel." Daniel's voice softened as he spoke her name. "Please. I know you don't want to go on like this. Feeling nothing but hatred. This isn't you. The woman I remember didn't enjoy hurting people."

Her form wavered, flickering in and out as she billowed up then drew back, making it look as if the very air was breathing. Her gaze swung to the flames dancing just above the opening of the garbage can.

Daniel stepped closer, signaling to Arrynn to move. She slowly sidestepped, watching to see if Isabel would attack, but the ghost seemed fixated on Daniel.

Daniel sighed. "Let us help you. Once you cross over, you'll be at peace. Happy."

She growled at Daniel's last word, flickering in and out, again. "I'll never be *happy*, and you'll never be free."

She raced at them, disappearing into a blast of flames as Arrynn tossed the picture into the can, the edges quickly catching fire. An echoing cry faded into the hiss of the paper as the picture turned to ash.

Arrynn slumped against the counter, smiling when Daniel walked over to her. Pain creased his forehead as he glanced at the smoking remains of the photograph.

She reached for him, gently taking his hand in hers. "I'm sorry. I know this isn't easy for you. Hell, it's torture."

He shrugged, though she could tell by the tight press of his lips and the way his other hand fisted then released at his side he was masking whatever true emotions he felt. "I just hate seeing her suffer. Get lost in the anger and hatred. Can't imagine anyone would want to live on like that—ghost or not."

"She's too far gone to realize that."

He nodded, turning to face Tanner as the man limped over to them. Daniel gave him a pat on his arm. "Thanks."

Tanner shook his head. "For what it's worth, I'm sorry, too. Having to dispatch her like this... Wouldn't wish it on my worst enemy. But I'm glad she's gone."

Daniel snorted. "Not quite, but one step closer."

Tanner furrowed his brow. "What do you mean by 'not quite'? I thought once you destroyed their connection, it sent them packing? For good."

"It does, but that photo and ticket wasn't the last link she had to our side of the veil. There's one more at my place. One last way in." He glanced at Arrynn. "And I have a feeling, it'll be harder than any of the others to destroy.

Isabel knows we're close to dispatching her. Once we cross that threshold, she's going to fight us every chance she gets."

Tanner stepped between them before Arrynn could answer. "Then, let's kick her ass for good."

Arrynn chuckled. "Help burn one talisman, and you're a converted ghost hunter. Thanks, Tanner, but you need to get Garret to the hospital. Unless you need one of us to drive you there."

Tanner scoffed at her. "Seriously, Arrynn? Been on my own since I was fourteen. Think I can manage to get my partner to the hospital. But he'd have my ass if he knew taking him there risked your lives."

"We can handle this. It's what we do. We'll be fine."

"Right. So, the dried blood on both of you—"

"Is part of the job." She gave Tanner a shove. "Christ, Tanner. We've got this. Thanks for the help but get Garret and get to the damn hospital before Daniel and I insist on taking you both there personally."

"I don't need a hospital. But I'd take a damn drink."

They turned as Garret's raspy voice sounded in the room. He stood at the doorway, noticeably resting his weight against the frame. He took a step forward, tripping against a chair as his legs seemed to buckle slightly.

"Fuck, Garret." Tanner raced over, shouldering his buddy's weight as he slid his arm under the other man's. "You're going to knock yourself out, again." Tanner sighed, glancing at them. "You two sure you got this? I mean, I know it's what you do, but... There's no shame in needing a bit of help."

Daniel slung his arm around Arrynn's shoulder. "Piece of cake."

She snorted. "What my partner said. Go. We'll head over to Daniel's and finish this."

Tanner nodded. "Fine. We'll go make sure Garret's head is somewhat okay. But do me a favor? Wait until morning. Get some rest. Heal. But face this fresh. Betting the sunlight wouldn't hurt, either."

Daniel huffed. "The longer we wait, the angrier she gets."

Arrynn palmed his chest. "They have a point." She silenced his protest with a finger across his lips. "She's bound to your house. She can't hurt anyone, and we could use the time to recuperate. Make a strategy." She smiled up at him. "She's not going anywhere. A few hours won't change that."

"Fine. We'll rest, but come sunrise...she's crossing over, one way or another."

He moved away, his displeasure mirrored in the rigid line of his back. Arrynn released a weary breath following the group out. They helped Tanner get Garret into their SUV, waving them off as they headed down the road. She glanced at Daniel as they slid into her vehicle. Some of the tension had lifted, though she could tell he wasn't happy about waiting.

She nudged him. "You okay?"

"Fine." He carded his hand through his hair. "So, where are we going, seeing as my house isn't an option?"

Arrynn backed up, checking the road before pulling out. "My place."

Daniel coughed. "You know, in all the time we've worked together, I've never been to your place. Was starting to think either you didn't want me there, or you lived at the center."

"I would have offered, but..." She smiled at him. "I knew I'd never want you to leave, so..." She looked back at the road. "Perhaps you should decide, now, whether you want to go there or not."

Daniel's mouth tipped up into a wicked grin. "Can't wait to see it."

CHAPTER TWELVE

Daniel tried to remain calm as Arrynn pulled into the driveway of a small cottage not too far from his house. He hadn't been joking. He'd honestly started to wonder if the reason she'd never had him over was because she simply stayed at Threshold. But, as she stuck her car into first, turned off the engine and got out, he knew he'd been lying to himself. He'd figured she hadn't invited him because she'd secretly known he had feelings for her and was doing her best not to have to tell him they weren't reciprocated.

He raked his hand through his hair. He'd come close to telling her he'd fallen in love with her. Hell, he'd had to bite back the words when she'd joked about it. Push the feelings so deep he wouldn't let the phrase slip. But, sitting in the car, staring at her house—he wasn't sure he could hold back. Not after everything they'd gone through. After allowing her to break through his walls.

He groaned inwardly. If he were honest, he was more afraid that she didn't feel that same. That he was a convenient distraction from the pain, the stress. That once they'd dispatched Isabel for good, Arrynn would realize he wasn't worth her efforts. That he was damaged goods.

Mixed emotions warred inside his head as he stepped out of the car and followed her up the short pathway to the front door. He looked down, grinning at the mat positioned in front of the entrance. "Seriously, sweetheart?"

She opened the door, glancing at him as she walked inside and flicked on the lights. "What?"

"You have a binding sigil as a welcome mat?"

Her smile lit up the entire night. "A girl can't be too careful about who, or what, she lets through her front door. Not when she knows monsters are real."

"Are you sure you want me to come in, then? Because once I cross this threshold, there's no going back. No pretending it was a couple of convenient hookups."

Arrynn's eyes widened, her teeth snagging her bottom lip. Uncertainty clouded her expression, for a moment, before heat bled through. She released a long breath, her stance clearly indicating she'd made some sort of decision. "I think it's a bit overdue, don't you? Besides, we already crossed that line last week. This is just reconfirming it wasn't one of those mistakes you talked about."

Daniel stepped forward, grabbing Arrynn around the waist as he kicked the door shut behind him. Then, he lifted her up, spinning until he had her pinned to the wall. He captured her gasp of surprise with his mouth, tasting the sweet essence that was uniquely her. Arrynn's fingers tunneled into his hair as he eased back, resting his forehead on hers.

He savored the moment, knowing it would be over far

too soon. "The only mistake was not having the balls to do this earlier."

"You had your reasons."

"None of which seem all that important from where I'm standing."

"You're here, now. That seems more important to me."

He grinned. "You need to stop doing that."

"Doing what?"

"Making me fall even harder for you than I already have. I'm already on the verge of screwing this up by admitting too much, too soon."

All the tension bled out of her shoulders as she leaned into him. "I don't scare easily, Daniel. Pretty damn sure there's nothing you could say to me that would make me run."

"Nothing?"

"Nothing that involves you planning on being in my life for the foreseeable future—and as more than just my damn hunting partner."

"Point noted. Then, I guess it's safe to do this." He hiked her up on his shoulder, giving her butt a slap as he turned, striding across the open room.

She laughed, bouncing against him as he paused at the hallway. "Second door on the right."

Daniel didn't slow as he headed for her room, taking them straight to the bed. He placed her on the edge of the mattress then toed off his boots. She reached for him as he came over her, taking his mouth with hers. His weight pressed her into the bed, but she wrapped her arms around his neck when he tried to shift onto his elbows.

Her breath feathered across his neck as he kissed a path along her jaw. "Don't. I like feeling you on top of me.

It feels right. Safe." She sighed. "Not that I need you to make me feel safe, I just..."

He silenced her with another kiss, this one coaxing. Inviting. She joined in, turning it more desperate. Raw. Her nails dug into his scalp as she tangled her fingers in his hair, as if needing the hold to ground herself.

He moaned at the slight sting, nipping at her jaw. "Letting someone in doesn't make you weak, sweetheart. Courageous, yeah. But not weak."

"Does that mean you'll finally take down those walls you've built around you? I've tried scaling them, but I keep losing my footing." She released a slow breath. "I see. You're more of a talker than a doer."

He chuckled. "What I *am* is crazy about you. And, if it takes putting my heart on the line to prove it... Guess I'm up for the job. But I won't accept anything less than yours in return. Or are you all talk, too?"

"I let you in the front door, didn't I?"

He grinned, claiming her mouth then working at stripping her down, reminding himself not to ruin her clothes in his need to touch her skin. Feel the silky flesh brush over his. Taste how excited he made her. He shuffled enough to tug her pants down her legs. He tossed them and her boots and socks onto the floor, leaving her in just her panties and top. He stared down at her, wondering if there'd ever be a time when his need for her didn't burn beneath his skin. Made it hard to think. To breathe. When his every thought wasn't shaded in the blue of her eyes or the chocolate hue of her hair. When his very soul wasn't connected to hers.

He sighed, fairly certain that day didn't exist. He was bound to her as surely as Isabel was bound to the ticket.

Only with Arrynn, it was based on love. Trust. A leap of faith, in a sense. She'd given him a second chance at life. At love. The thought eased any lingering worries. He'd didn't need to know if Arrynn felt the same way. All he needed to do was love her.

Arrynn smoothed her finger along his brow while hers creased into a vee. "You okay?"

"At this moment? Perfect."

"Then, why are you looking at me like that?"

"Like what?"

"Like you've never seen me before."

He reached forward, brushing his fingers along her jaw. "Maybe I'm just seeing us in a new way. But that can wait until after I've made you scream."

He claimed her mouth, again, tugging and lifting at her shirt—barely parting enough to somehow yank it over her head while she made short work of his. It took a bit of maneuvering, but he managed to strip off her bra and panties. He kissed a path down her neck, dropping lower to nip at one of her nipples.

Arrynn tugged at his hair. "No teasing. I need you inside me."

He scraped his teeth along the taut bud, loving the way she shivered in response. "Soon, sweetheart. After I taste you. Have you come all over my tongue."

"Next time, Daniel, I promise. But now…" She gave a sharp pull, gaining his attention as his head snapped up. "I need you inside me. Pounding me. Fucking me like there might not be a tomorrow."

Because there might not be.

He pushed away the thought. There'd be a tomorrow. And several million after that where her life was concerned. Of that, he was certain.

Daniel sighed in defeat, moving back up her body. He grabbed hold of her as he rolled onto his back, smiling at her sharp inhalation. "Then, ride me, Arrynn. Take what you need. Make your pussy cream my cock, because once you've climaxed, I'm flipping you over and claiming your ass. Gonna show you that I have no intentions of letting you put it in jeopardy. But only if you want me to. If you agree this is so much more than me fucking away this past week. I need it to mean more."

Arrynn's breath hitched, a deep flush shading her skin before she levered onto her knees. She leaned toward the edge of the bed, sliding open the drawer on the small side table before placing a tube of lubricant on the mattress beside them. She gave him a gut-wrenching smile then grasped the base of his cock as it pulsed against his stomach. She licked her lips, looking as if she was going to swallow him first, then wedged his shaft between her legs. She trailed the head up and down her cleft, mixing her arousal with his before lodging him at her sex. She palmed his chest, bridging her weight on him as she slowly sank down, immersing him inside her wet heat.

Her head tilted back, a husky moan breaking free. "God, Daniel. So damn big. So hard." Her head bowed forward as she levered up, keeping only the crown snugged within her before dropping, again. Harder. Faster. "Need you."

Daniel fisted her hair, holding it back as he stared at her. "All yours, Arrynn. Whatever you need...it's yours."

Tears pooled in her eyes, a few making their way along her cheeks as she smiled at him, lifting one hand to touch his jaw. He kissed her palm, shifting her hand back to his chest when she slammed down, taking him deeper. She kept moving, this time, seemingly losing herself in the steady rise and fall of her body. Her eyes drifted shut, her jaw tensing as she rode his cock.

He smoothed his hands along her thighs, promising himself he'd spend the next round touching every inch of her. Memorizing every subtle change in her skin. How she felt beneath his fingers, his lips, his tongue. But, for now...

He placed his hands on her ass, helping her move, loving how her muscles flexed as her orgasm neared. How the flush on her skin pinkened. She tried to increase her pace, and her breathing roughened, a strangled cry echoing around them.

He stilled her movements, thrusting up into her quivering pussy, pushing her completely over. Her head fell back, her nails digging into his flesh as her release covered his shaft, the steady contractions of her walls nearly taking him with her.

He watched her climax, memorizing every twitch of her lips, every mumbled gasp that seemed wrenched from her chest before he levered up and rolled her onto her back as her knees splayed around his thighs. He rocked onto his heels, his cock still buried inside her as he uncapped the lube and covered two of his fingers in the slick fluid. Her gaze held his as he slowly pulled his shaft free, circling her tight pucker then sinking one finger inside her ass. She gasped, pressing up into the penetration, begging him to just fuck her already.

He waved off her request, refusing to alter his pace as he finger-fucked her ass, gradually loosening the tight muscles. When some of the clenching seemed to ease, he added a second finger, loving the way she writhed on the bed, sweat beading her skin, her eyes squeezed shut. Her hands finally landed on his arms, her nails scoring his flesh as she looked at him, the rawness in her eyes telling him all he needed to know.

He removed his fingers, smiling at her raspy huff before grabbing the lube, again. He drew a few lines of the fluid down his shaft, covering his length. Then, he placed the head of his cock at her entrance, firmly pressing against the tight ring of muscles. He eased forward, watching her face for any indication the pressure was too intense. A guttural moan rumbled from her chest as he popped through the tight ring of muscles and slowly slid inside.

He stopped as his balls slapped against her ass. "Shit, Arrynn. So damn hot and tight. Are you okay?"

She nodded, moaning his name when he pulled back then pushed in.

He paused, thumbing her jaw until she focused on him, the blue in her eyes nothing but a thin ring. "Talk to me, sweetheart. Is this too much?"

She shook her head then cursed when he tsked at her. "Fine, just...damn, so intense." She nipped at his finger, then licked it. "Move, Daniel. For the love of god, just move."

He placed one hand on the mattress beside her chest as the other held her thigh. He wanted to watch his cock plunge inside her. Watch how every thrust sent a wave of reaction across her body—tensing her muscles. Beading her nipples into tight, hard buds. Making her hands fist and release. The lines in her neck corded as she arched up, heels locked behind his back, head pushed into the bed.

"Oh god, Daniel. Yes!"

Her voice hissed into a cry as her ass clamped around him, more contractions rippling along his cock.

"Shit, sweetheart. Can't..."

He pounded into her, knowing he'd be disappointed in his loss of control but unable to stop. The smooth glide of her skin, the steady rasp of his name pushed him over. He tightened his grip, holding her still as he made a dozen more passes before the tingling sensation in his sac finally shot forward.

"Arrynn! Fuck!"

He stiffened, his shaft emptying inside her in a series of hard jerks. Each spurt set his nerves on fire until he collapsed over her, chest heaving, muscles quivering. Arrynn wrapped her arms around his back, holding him tight. Her body shook through the last of her release, her face damp against his cheek.

He found the strength to push to his elbows, frowning at the moisture coating her skin. "Arrynn?"

She gave him a smile, her eyes drifting closed. "Not hurt, just..." She sighed. "I don't know, really."

"It's been a hell of a week. Seems reasonable we're both feeling a bit on edge. That, and I did just make you come. Hard."

She swatted his arm. "You shouted my name fairly loud, yourself."

"Hell, yeah. I'm spent." He got to his feet, offering her his hand. "What do you say to a super quick shower then sleep?"

"You promise to do all the work, because I'm not sure I can move."

"Thinking that can be arranged."

She pointed at their clothes when he went to pick her up. "We should probably plug in our cells. Isabel drained everything at Tanner's. And, as much as I'd love some uninterrupted sleep, I did tell Tanner to call once he and Garret were done at the hospital."

Daniel nodded, rummaging through their stuff until he had both phones. He plugged them in then turned to her. "Anything else?"

"Just your arms around me for the rest of the night."

"Shower, first, but deal."

He laughed, lifting her up. She wrapped her arms around his neck, kissing his jaw as he covered the short space. He placed her on her feet as he twisted on the taps. He grabbed a couple of towels from the shelf beside the stall, waiting for the water to heat before leading her in. She didn't say much, just stood there, watching him as he cleaned her then grabbing the soap and returning the favor. Her hands seemed to tremble slightly as she finished up, staring at him once he'd rinsed and cut off the water.

She palmed his chest when he went to open the glass door. "Daniel, I—"

He silenced her with a quick kiss. "We're both exhausted. Tell me in the morning, when I know it's not fatigue or great sex talking."

She snickered. "You don't even know what I was going to say."

"But I know what I want to say. So, humor me."

She shook her head, giving him a kiss before stepping out. She glanced back at him when he smoothed his hand along her hip, giving her ass a squeeze. "Give me a couple of days to recover, and you can have it, again."

"A couple... Fuck, I hurt you."

"Damn it, Daniel, have you ever stuck something up your ass?" She snorted at his expression. "Figured as much. You didn't hurt me, but it was...intense. And I won't lie. I'll feel you tomorrow, but in a good way. It'll remind me of how you looked. How you couldn't seem to get enough of me."

"There's no *seem* about it. You're definitely a habit I don't think I'll be able to break."

She arched her brow. "Thought we were waiting until the morning to get all sappy?"

"Pretty sure you started it."

"Did not—"

A sharp blare of music cut her off.

Daniel walked into the bedroom, Arrynn in tow as he stopped at the side table. "It's Tanner, but... Guess they got in to see a doctor pretty quick."

He swiped his finger across the glass. "I'll give you this much, Tanner, you have impeccable timing. How's Garret?"

"Cartwright? Thank, Christ. I've been trying to get you for damn near twenty minutes. Fuck, thought you two were dead."

"Trying? Dead?"

"Just...shut up for a second. Where the hell are you?"

"I'm with Arrynn. At her place. Why?"

"Shit! I knew it."

"Knew what? Damn it, Tanner, you're not making any sense."

Tanner's breath sounded on the other end as the man mumbled something. "I told Garret you'd never fucking call us back after insisting we leave, but...he was worried you two had merely brushed us off. Decided to hunt that bitch down tonight. Then, we got that damn call…"

Daniel held the phone out, putting it on speaker when Arrynn mouthed questions at him. "Call? What call? Where the hell are you?"

"Your place. And I'm pretty sure we just fucked up."

A numbing cold settled in Daniel's gut. He looked over at Arrynn, his fear reflected in her eyes. Daniel inhaled, trying to keep calm as he began gathering his clothes. "You're at my place? As in the one place Isabel has complete access to?"

"Don't fucking patronize me. I know how idiotic this sounds, but… When a fellow hunter—hell, a friend—calls you begging for help, you answer it. Even if you think you're being set up."

Daniel glanced at Arrynn as she shimmied into her pants. "You're right. And I appreciate that you two broke ranks to go to my house, despite everything that's happened. At least, tell me you're armed."

Tanner snorted. "We're not stupid. Stopped at an all-night gas station. Took every container of salt they had. Couldn't find anything made of iron, though. Luckily, I still had the frying pan in the SUV. When we got here and saw that truck parked out front, figured someone was home."

"Truck? What truck? I own a Renegade."

"Shit if we know, but there's a red Chevy off to the side of your driveway."

"Christ. That sounds like Jimmy's."

Tanner cleared his throat. "Are you trying to tell me a ghost had his truck all this time?"

"It was more important to Jimmy, but... Doesn't matter. Where are you now?"

"Standing in a damn circle of salt near your kitchen. Gotta admit, Danno, we're feeling pretty naked just sitting here, waiting for your ghost to show."

"Trust me, she's already there." He juggled the phone as he yanked his shirt on then tugged on his boots. "Did Garret have enough time to get his head checked before you bolted?"

"Since when do ERs do anything quickly? We'd just walked through the damn doors when my cell rang. Wouldn't have answered it, but it was Arrynn's number." His voice huffed through the phone. "I swear to god it was her voice. Said you'd gone to hunt Isabel and had gotten waylaid. You were bleeding out, and she was trapped. There was a jumble of static and interference, and a whole lot of screaming in the background before the line went dead. Tried calling you both back, but never got through until you picked up, just now. Drove over here expecting a repeat of Jimmy's place." He sighed. "While we're pissed it's a setup, we're glad neither of you are in pieces on the floor."

Arrynn moved in close as she spoke over the phone. "Powerful ghosts can mimic voices. Especially if they've had three years to practice. And the fact she's able to manipulate your phone... It's not unheard of, but it does mean she's far stronger than we imagined. Explains why she's still kicking our asses."

"But why get us over here? If she's as smart as you say, surely she realizes you two would eventually return. She has to know you'll come after that photo."

"That's the point. She wants us there on her terms.

When she's prepared, not us. And she knows we'll do whatever it takes to save you."

Tanner snorted. "Don't need saving. But some backup would be nice. You two dressed and out the door, yet?"

"We're on our way, just...stay in the circle."

"Trust me, we're not going anywhere. At least the power's on, and we have lights. Not sure how long that will last. But, once you two get here...we're taking this bitch down. One way or another."

The line went dead.

Arrynn cursed under her breath. "So much for some sleep. And what the hell is up with Jimmy's truck? Isabel shouldn't be able to manipulate it."

Daniel shrugged. "No idea. But we'll fix this. Get Garret and Tanner out of there and burn that photograph."

She nodded, tossing him the keys as she headed for the passenger side. Daniel slipped into the vehicle, started the engine and headed out. He didn't like the way this was shaping up. Tanner. Garret...Arrynn. Anyone who meant anything to him was in the line of fire, and he wasn't sure he could save them all before they all went up in flames.

CHAPTER THIRTEEN

"That's definitely Jimmy's truck."

Arrynn glanced at Daniel as he pulled into his driveway, parking beside the red vehicle. "I'm confused, too, but...let's focus on Tanner and Garret. On burning that picture. If this wasn't Isabel's doing, we can take care of it, after."

His jaw tensed as he slapped his hand on the steering wheel. "You know as well as I do that she shouldn't have any connection to Jimmy's truck. That..." He pointed at the vehicle. "That could be a new kind of trouble."

"Agreed, but I'm not sure we can do anything about it, other than be watchful."

He nodded, snagging her wrist when she went to jump out. "This wasn't how I wanted tonight to end. You know that, right? I wanted to spend the rest of the night holding you. Wake up the same way."

"Guess Tanner isn't the only one who has impeccable timing."

Daniel frowned. "If it weren't for Tanner and Garret... I can't let her harm anyone else. Not because of me."

"She'd be harming folks, regardless. She's not Isabel. She's a vengeful spirit, Daniel. It's what they do."

"I know that, but..." He sighed, raking a hand through his hair. "Just promise me one thing. If things go south in there, you'll get Tanner and Garret and leave. No matter what."

"You mean leave you behind."

"Arrynn..."

"No. No fucking way. Lovers aside...we were partners, first. That hasn't changed."

"The hell it hasn't. Just because I haven't had the guts to tell you I love you, doesn't make it any less of a fact." He reefed open the door, glancing back at her over his shoulder. "Whether you love me in return doesn't matter. And I won't lose you to my past. Period."

Arrynn huffed, exiting the car and darting around to the front in order to catch up to Daniel. "Stop, just... Fuck!" She moved in front of him and shoved at his chest with one finger as she leaned in close. "You cannot tell me you love me while we're in the midst of a damn ghost hunt then turn away as if you didn't just blow me out of the water." She smoothed her palm on his jacket as he covered her hand with his. "What am I supposed to think?"

His expression softened. "Pretty simple, sweetheart. That I love you."

"But how can I be sure it's not the adrenaline or the fear of failing or—"

He silenced her with a finger across her lips. "Because I've been falling for you since that day we met. If having

Isabel return gave me the balls to finally tell you, so be it. But how I feel is all about you. Not the circumstances." He nodded at the house. "Now, how about we go help Tanner and Garret before they get any heroic ideas in their thick skulls and decide to step outside that damn circle of salt?"

Arrynn's mouth gaped open as he stepped around her, heading for the front door. Her pulse sounded in her ears as her heart thrashed against her ribs. He'd said he loved her. That it had nothing to do with ghosts or thinking he might not see the sun rise.

She cursed at the shakiness in her gait as followed after him. He didn't seem the least bit unnerved by his admission as he signaled her, mouthing the countdown before opening the door. The rush of air swirled what remained of the sigil he'd inscribed into the air, the chalky dust spreading out across the room. Daniel scanned each direction then drew himself up. He seemed calm. Too calm. As if he'd made a decision, only Arrynn was pretty sure it wasn't one she'd approve of.

His words from outside replayed in her mind. He was willing to sacrifice himself if that's what it took to finally dispatch Isabel. And Arrynn wasn't sure she'd be able to stop him if things got messy.

He met her gaze, not even a hint of fear in his eyes. "We'll make sure Tanner and Garret are safe, first, then we'll retrieve the photo."

She nodded her agreement. "Where is it?"

"In a box in the attic."

"Why is everything always in an attic or a fucking basement? Doesn't anyone just keep shit in a closet in the bedroom, anymore?"

He chuckled. "Damn, I love you. Ready?"

"Daniel... Shit."

He didn't acknowledge her as he struck off toward the rear of the house, salt in one hand, tire iron in the other. Arrynn watched his back, constantly checking behind them as he walked through the kitchen. Tanner and Garret looked up when they entered the main living room, relief washing over their faces.

Tanner grinned. "You know, if we keep meeting up like this, the director's going to suggest we partner up or something."

Daniel snorted. "We don't have to hug, now, do we? Had any visitors?"

"Nothing. Which I'll admit freaks me out even more. Hell, she hasn't even drained the power, yet." Tanner moved outside the ring, nodding at Daniel when he gave Garret an iron rod. "For the record, I don't know how you guys do this shit. All the hiding and semi-transparent stuff. Only having salt and a damn tire iron as defense. Give me a straight up fight with a blood-crazed shifter any day."

"You get used to it. Besides, I had a great teacher." Daniel winked at her. Fucking winked, as if they weren't about to face a deadly spirit. "Don't suppose you two would consider sitting the rest of this out?"

Garret snorted. "Didn't hit my head near hard enough for that. Figure I owe your ghost a beating."

"It's a ghost. You can't beat them, but...with any luck, we can send her over. For good, this time."

Garret nodded, joining them outside the circle. "Just tell us what you need."

Daniel glanced at her. "If I said to grab Arrynn and lock

her in your SUV?" He grunted when she punched him in the shoulder. "Fine. What we need is in the attic. It's accessed though a hatch in the hallway. Hoping Tanner can give me a boost up. I'll find the photo and burn it."

"All while fending off Isabel on your own? I don't think so. It took all of us back at the apartment, and she's bound to be even angrier, now." Arrynn turned, looking at them over her shoulder. "I'm going up, too. Period."

She stopped when the lights throughout the house flickered then winked out, leaving nothing but the light of the moon brightening the shadows. "Shit."

Tanner snorted. "At least, your ghost is consistent."

"It also means she's fueling herself." Arrynn grabbed a Maglite from her pocket, cursing when it didn't turn on. "And she's drained our equipment, too."

"So, how the hell do we fight her?"

Daniel stepped in front. "Our eyes will adjust. Nothing's changed. We still need the photo, which means we need to get inside the attic."

Daniel struck off, glancing back once as he made his way down the hall. She followed behind him, checking each room as they passed the open door, ensuring nothing would surprise them. Her breath caught as she looked into Daniel's bedroom, the handcuffs on the bed glinting in the moonlight. A chuckle sounded behind her, but she just flipped off Tanner and Garret, moving in behind Daniel as he stopped beneath a panel in the ceiling.

He turned to Tanner. "Thinking we'll go up, toss you the box once we find it. Then, we'll all head outside and burn the contents."

Tanner nodded, lacing his hands together as he bent in front of Daniel. "We'll be waiting."

Daniel placed his foot in Tanner's hand, knocking the panel aside before pulling himself up.

Arrynn looked at them. "You guys sure you'll be okay?"

Garret waved his tire iron in the air as he held up a box of salt. "Armed and pissed. We'll make another circle of salt so you have a safe place to land once you're done. Just be sure you finish this."

Daniel extended his hand. "Come on."

She reached for him, using Tanner's help to boost her into the cramped space. She shivered as the air cooled around them. "Getting cold in here, suddenly."

"I know. She's here, just...waiting." He scanned the dark room. "Going to be hard to find shit in the dark. I can't see my own damn hand."

"They might not last long, but I brought some countermeasures."

She slung her shotgun on her shoulder as she reached into the bag secured around her waist, fishing out a couple of glow sticks. She cracked them, grinning at the neon light that filled the space. "These won't be as easy to drain."

"Nicely played. Now, to find that damn box with her pictures in it."

Daniel stepped forward when his breath condensed into a wispy cloud. Arrynn inhaled sharply when Isabel appeared in a rush of white mist, grabbing Daniel and slamming him against the low ceiling. He swung his tire iron, landing hard on the floor when the strike caused her to dissipate.

Arrynn knelt beside him. "You okay?"

"Starting to get real tired of her tossing me around."

"Hard to avoid it when she can pop up before we have a chance to react." Arrynn handed him a small container. "Here. Sprinkle this on your arms, legs and neck. The iron filings should burn her if she tries to touch you again."

He cocked an eyebrow at her. "What about you?"

"Not enough. And she seems more interested in you, right now."

"Arrynn—"

"This isn't up for debate. You know I'm right. You just don't want to admit it."

He muttered under his breath but did as she'd suggested. "This means I'm going for the box. Once I find it, I'll toss it over."

"I'll keep her busy."

Daniel frowned but straightened, heading toward the boxes lining one of the far walls. The ghost appeared, again, shrieking when she touched Daniel's skin. Her eyes glowed red as she swirled upward, vanishing through the ceiling.

He stopped at the wall, eyeing the boxes. He placed his tire iron on the floor as he picked up the first box. "Wish I knew which one it was in, but...pretty much just tossed these up here. I'll go as fast as I can."

Arrynn scanned the room, her breath appearing in small bursts in front of her face. She shivered as the temperature dropped further, the hairs on her nape prickling.

"Mine!"

The word thundered through the attic a moment before Isabel exploded into the room, her ghostly form expanding outwards. Arrynn tossed salt at her, managing to get off a round from the shotgun before the ghost disappeared. But Isabel seemed to counter Arrynn's efforts, disappearing then reappearing in another spot seamlessly. Arrynn did her best to strike before the ghost had a chance to launch a full attack, but each shift got faster until Isabel's icy grip tightened around Arrynn's throat.

She inhaled, kicking her feet as the ghost lifted her off the floor, those blood-red eyes glaring at Arrynn.

Isabel hissed. "He'll never be yours. Never be free."

Arrynn tried to position her weapon when Daniel's tire iron struck Isabel, scattering her into a white mist as it hit the wall then fell to the floor. Arrynn dropped, gasping in some air as she reached for the metal rod. Her fingers closed around it just as Isabel reappeared, grasping her neck, again. The ghost lifted her up, the tire iron slipping out of Arrynn's grasp. The scenery started to dim when an unholy cry filled the room as white particles covered her skin. Arrynn dropped to the floor, gasping in air as she coughed in an effort to breathe. Firm hands wrapped around her, drawing her backwards.

Daniel held her close. "Breathe, sweetheart. Just focus on breathing."

Arrynn tried to shove him off. "Get...box." She groaned as those few words seemed to gouge her throat.

"You're more important."

"She'll kill all of us, if..." She coughed, again, clutching at her neck.

"Shit!"

Daniel stood, grabbing the remaining boxes. He tossed each one at the opening. "We'll just burn the whole fucking lot of them." He moved back over to the access panel. "You guys ready? I've got six coming toward you."

Tanner's grunt sounded muffled from below. "Just toss them down, already."

Daniel pushed each one over the edge then turned to her. "I'll lower you down. Then, we head outside and build a damn bonfire."

She nodded, landing inside the circle of salt as Garret steadied her.

He ran his fingers over her neck. "Fuck, Arrynn. Even in the dark, I can see the bruises."

She waved him off as Daniel jumped down beside her. "I'll heal. But she's not going to make this easy." She nodded at Daniel. "Nice toss back there. Gave me a chance to catch my breath."

"Toss? What…" His voice trailed off as a form started to take shape in front of them before winking out.

Arrynn shook her head. At least, Isabel seemed drained. Arrynn motioned to the boxes. "Thinking we should each take one. Daniel and I can take two. Whoever makes it out first starts the fire."

The men nodded, each picking up a box. Daniel handed her two, frowning as his gaze strayed to her neck. He didn't speak, just took a deep breath then darted off, running down the hallway. Tanner motioned her to follow, muttering something about him and Garret bringing up the rear.

She moved as fast as she could, shouting Daniel's name when Isabel appeared between them, grabbing Daniel and tossing him through one of the windows at the back. Arrynn dropped her boxes, swinging her weapon off her shoulder and unloading a round of salt. The ghost misted into nothing.

Arrynn yelled at Tanner and Garret to pick up her

share as she raced outside, kneeling beside Daniel as he rolled onto his back on the porch. She brushed pieces of glass off his clothes, wincing at the laceration across his forehead. "Shit. Are you okay?"

He grunted, taking a few tries to push onto his hands and knees. "Thought that shit only happened in the movies. Christ, it hurts."

"You should stay here. Let us—"

"No way. I'll be fine. We just need to get clear—*Look out!*"

He grabbed her shoulders, launching them both sideways off the porch as Isabel rushed toward them. They hit the ground hard, pain sparking through her body. She blinked when Tanner and Garret appeared over them. Garret cinched his fingers around her wrist, yanking her upright before slipping his arm around her back. Tanner did the same with Daniel, half carrying them across the sandy grass until the reached another circle of salt.

Tanner shook his head, looking at where Isabel hovered over the boxes, face morphing between varying stages of decay. "This is fucked. We can't take more than a few steps before she's on us."

Daniel eased free of Tanner's hold, gazing at Arrynn. "He's right. She's just too damn strong. We need some kind of distraction." He glanced back at the ghost then sighed. "It worked at the apartment. If I draw her off—"

"Forget it." Tanner huffed when Daniel glared at him. "You're not damn well sacrificing yourself for nothing. We had to leave those other boxes inside the house just to get you guys to safety. No way anything you do will occupy her long enough to get back inside."

"Then, we'll burn the whole fucking house down."

Arrynn touched his arm. "Daniel…"

"It's just a thing."

"Everything you own is inside that house."

"That's all just stuff. What's important to me—what matters—is standing inside this circle. As long I don't lose that, I don't care about the rest."

Tanner groaned. "Fuck, we are going to end up hugging, aren't we? Fine. Is that gasoline jug I saw on the porch full?"

Daniel nodded. "More than enough to do the job."

"Perfect. We'll both distract her while Garret and Arrynn douse the back porch with accelerant then set the bitch on fire."

Daniel looked as if he was going to argue before simply nodding. He gave her shoulder a squeeze. "Be careful. And don't worry about anything other than starting that fire."

She moved to answer when he gave her a quick kiss. He winked, stepping outside the circle with Tanner as they moved toward the house until Isabel raced at them. The men backed up, countering the ghost's first attack with a blast of salt.

Arrynn tugged on Garret's sleeve. "Let's go while she's recharging."

They took off, reaching the edge of the porch when the apparition burst into form in front of them, knocking them both back. They rolled across the grass, landing several feet away.

Garret groaned. "Shit, she's relentless. I've killed an entire pack of werewolves far easier than this."

"Hard to kill what's not really there."

Arrynn stood, cocking her weapon when the ghost shimmered into view. It looked beyond her shoulder then disappeared. A searing cold chilled the back of Arrynn's neck, but there was only empty space when she spun.

She rubbed the cold spot, nodding to Garret. "We should go."

They took two steps, only to stop when Isabel materialized on the porch, seemingly intent on keeping them from entering. Daniel and Tanner moved in beside them.

Daniel shook his head. "She won't stick with us. Keeps leaving when you two get close."

Arrynn sighed. "Then, we hit her with everything we've got, tip over the jug and toss a lighter at it. Hope enough catches fire."

Tanner scoffed. "Leave it up to chance? I don't like the sound of that. There's got to be another way to destroy her."

Arrynn scoffed. "We can ask her to go nicely. Daniel's tried. Hasn't worked so far."

"That's it?"

"That's why we hunt vengeful spirits. Harder than hell to get rid of."

"Well, this night just keeps getting better." Tanner kicked at the ground. "Fine, we do what you said. Hit her or whatever, start a fire out here and hope for the best."

Daniel drew himself up. "I'll go for the gasoline canister. I'll light it, one way or another."

Arrynn snagged his arm. "I don't like the sound of that."

"I'll be careful, just... Shit, here she comes."

Isabel hissed, heading toward them when the air in front chilled, a gray mist slowly forming. Daniel held out his arm, holding back the others when a familiar silhouette materialized out of the air. The apparition seemed to waver then stabilize, standing its ground as Isabel suddenly halted, hovering several feet away.

Tanner gasped. "Holy shit, is that—"

"Jimmy." Arrynn glanced over at Daniel. "It's Jimmy."

The man turned slightly, giving them a salute before drawing himself up. He moved closer to Isabel. The other ghost retreated, seemingly unsure of what to do.

Jimmy stopped. "You said you wanted me, Isabel. So, you'll get me. All of me."

He bowed his head then raced forward. He hit Isabel full force, their energies exploding in a cluster of colored light before winking out. The charge in the air dimmed, the temperature gradually rising.

Tanner took a couple of steps forward, twisting to glance back at them, mouth gaped open, eyes wide. He waved at where the spirits had disappeared. "What the hell just happened?"

Daniel sighed, tugging Arrynn against his chest before wrapping his arms around her. "Jimmy just saved our asses."

"But how? I mean...wasn't he a ghost, too?"

"It's...complicated. In essence, they canceled each other out. Think of it as matter and anti-matter. A positive and a negative."

"So...that's it? No burning the picture, no more getting tossed around? She's just...gone?"

Daniel shrugged. "Arrynn and I will still burn it. Hell, I'll burn every damn photo, but...it won't change anything. She's gone. They both are."

Tanner scratched his head. "Fuck. I swear, if I never...

never have to hunt with you two, again, it'll be too soon. That...that's just weird shit."

"You hunt people who turn into werewolves. You don't think that's weird?"

"Hey, they're either human or shifted. None of this semi-transparent, but can toss you around, shit." Tanner joined them. "Garret and I will do one last sweep of your house, just to ease our conscience, while you two burn that stuff."

The men took off, tossing out the boxes they'd abandoned in the house. Daniel gathered them, piling them up before dousing them in gasoline. He flicked a lighter, igniting a piece of paper before setting the entire stack on fire.

Arrynn nudged him. "Didn't you want to see what was in the other ones?"

"I haven't looked in them since I moved here. Can't be that important. Besides, I'd rather work on making new memories. Ones worth saving."

She smiled, moving into his arms as he beckoned her. "I like the sound of that. Though, I am sorry it had to end this way. I can't imagine how much it hurts."

He dropped a kiss on the top of her head. "Not nearly as much as the prospect of losing you. That..." He coughed, the sound thick and raw. "Couldn't survive that. Even if you only want what we had before. Just as long as you're okay."

She snorted, gazing up at him. "Whatever happened to fighting for the woman you love? Surely, you won't give up before I tell you I love you, too?"

"I can't force you to..." He inhaled. "What did you say?"

"I see I've got your attention."

"You've always had it. Now, tell me what you just said."

"Didn't you hear me the first time?"

"Arrynn…" He cupped her chin. "Humor me. Please?"

"I said…I love you, too."

"About damn time."

He dipped low, taking her mouth in his. His tongue tangled with hers, the lazy strokes only making her want him more. She tunneled her fingers through his hair, anchoring them together. A throat cleared off to their left. Daniel eased back, glancing up at Tanner and Garret.

Tanner tsked. "Still jumping the gun. Don't you two have any restraint?" He shook his head. "House seems clear. Though with what you two deal with, all I can say is that there aren't any werewolves, vampires or humans inside. You'll have to deal with the spirit side of things."

Daniel's expression sobered. "I think we can handle that. Thanks for checking."

"No problem." Tanner nodded. "I take back what I said before. You two aren't pussies. You're fucking insane. And totally kick ass." He motioned to Garret. "Thinking we should go get Garret's head looked at for real, this time. Let you two get back to your handcuffs."

Arrynn rolled her eyes. "Jackass."

Tanner chuckled. "Glad to know Danno's putting his old life to good use." He turned, heading for their truck before glancing back at them. "Thinking you two deserve a day off. I'll let the director know. And I'll tell the man you need more salt. Like a warehouse full of it."

"Thanks. And Tanner…if you and Garret ever need backup…"

Tanner snorted. "I don't know, Danno. Hunting *weres* might seem tame after this. But I'll keep it in mind."

Daniel sighed, scooping her into his arms, laughing when she swatted his shoulder, insisting she could walk. "Humor me. And, for the record, Tanner might be a jackass, but I love the way he thinks. Because you, the handcuffs...thinking that's exactly how I want this evening to end. Especially after your declaration of undying love..."

She groaned, shaking her head. "Seriously? After everything we just went through, you want my *undying* love?"

He shrugged. "Some souls are worth taking the chance over. But I'm all for putting that off for the next seventy years, if it's all the same to you."

"Seventy, at the very least." She tightened her arms around his neck. "But I get to use the handcuffs, next."

"Oh, sweetheart. By the time I'm done, you won't have the strength to do anything other than fall asleep in my arms. But, on the chance you're still feisty...you're on."

"An angel?" Kei scrubbed a hand down his face as he tilted his head forward. "I summoned a fucking angel?"

Fire licked across his skin, the tiny arcs flashing bright in the darkness. Anger fueled the flames, burning the yellow wisps into a deep crimson. Of all the bloody screw ups...

Kei crossed the cemetery, stopping just shy of the symbol he'd inscribed on the ground. Black ash coated the parched dirt, traces of blood baked into the grooves scored on the land. He stared at the man crouched within the circle, muscles straining, skin gleaming in the moonlight. Creamy-white feathers fluttered in the breeze, his wings still unfurled across his back. Sweat beaded the guy's flesh, trailing down the strong curve of his spine. Summonings weren't pleasurable for demons. For angels —they killed more often than they succeeded.

Kei frowned. He'd cast a fire enchantment. Used more than a bit of his blood and all the damn power he could spare as payment. A desperate last effort to prolong his life, just long enough to hunt and kill the fallen bastard who'd cursed him to this fucking realm. The god damn human world. The one entity who could destroy this dimension and a dozen more like it if Kei didn't end the war before it began. He'd expected a blood demon. A soulless vessel he could possess until he'd found his prey. Preserve what little strength he had left before the final battle.

And he'd fucking deserved the creature. Fire enchantments were tricky. Risky. He would have gladly accepted death as a suitable recourse for a botched attempt. But he'd gotten every intonation and ancient pronunciation right. Had known the moment he'd finished, he'd been successful.

And yet, he'd somehow summoned an angel.

Kei crossed his arms over his chest as he braced his feet a shoulder width apart. "Don't suppose you're really a blood demon in disguise?"

The man's ragged breathing filled the air, his head finally lifting enough to meet Kei's gaze. Pain creased his forehead, his clear blue eyes wide with surprise.

Kei shook his head, leaning his hip against a tombstone. "Guess that's a no." He held up his hand, hoping to stop the guy when he looked as if he was going to try to stand. "I wouldn't do that just yet unless you like falling. Wouldn't want to bruise that pretty-boy face of yours."

The angelic man glared at him, pushing to his feet before stumbling across the circle. He hit one of the stone crosses, the dull thud echoing through the graveyard. He sagged against the headstone, anger coloring his eyes.

Kei tsked. "Can't say I didn't warn you."

"Silence, demon, before I strike you down for simply standing there."

Kei chuckled. "Yeah, you might find that whole smiting thing a bit difficult. Summonings tend to drain your life force. And I didn't use near enough energy to fuel an angel." He cocked his head to the side. "You got a name?"

The man clenched his jaw, drawing himself up despite the ways his limbs shook from the strain. "I'm an angel, not stupid. Names are powerful."

"Right. Because that's really what I'd been hoping for. A self-righteous asshole with enough soul to fill this godforsaken cemetery. That was my plan all along." He sighed. "The name's Kei."

"I don't care."

"Jackass it is."

The man sneered. "I won't fall for your tricks."

"No, you chose to fall from the fucking sky instead." Kei closed the distance, wondering when the guy would notice he was buck-ass nude. "How the hell did you get here, anyway? And what did you do with my demon?"

"What did I..." The man arched a brow, his wings fluttering against the stone as the wind picked up, tossing dried leaves into the air like confetti. "And here I thought you might be slightly more intelligent than most demons. You just said you summoned me. There's a blood token carved into the ground. You figure it out."

"I cast a fire enchantment. For a blood demon." Kei smirked. "I'll admit, ancient spells aren't my specialty, but even I'm not incompetent enough to fuck it up to the point I get an angel as compensation. Why are you really here? Who sent you?"

"Again. *You* summoned *me*."

"Are you deaf? I said I summoned a blood demon. Fuck!" Kei turned, taking a few angry steps away before spinning. "Why would I raise the one being who can't help me?"

"Since when do demons require help?"

Kei blew out an exasperated breath, twisting his palm face up before allowing his magic to spark to life. A flicking light appeared above his hand, the heat warning his skin. "Fire mage, jackass."

"You said you were a demon."

"I said I summoned one. You decided I was a demon." Kei allowed the flame to bounce in his hand before racing up his arm then down the other, finally winking out. The feel of his power soothed some of the rawness coursing through him, though the resulting wave of dizziness was just another reminder of how much energy he'd sacrificed. How weak he really was. "Don't suppose you'll surrender your soul long enough for me to possess your body—use you as a vessel to hunt down a nasty bastard that needs exterminating?"

The man shook his head, finally glancing down. Kei smiled. Despite the fact the guy was far too pure for his tastes, Kei had to admit he was more than attractive. Messy brown hair tousled about his head, strong smooth features that curved in perfect symmetry—the man was beautiful. Breathtaking, in fact. Even his body seemed flawless—pale skin covering lean muscles that flexed with every small movement. If it weren't for the fact the angel had been drained of his grace, Kei bet his ass the other man would be a tough opponent to best. That's if the guy would actually fight. Hell, who was he kidding? Without direction from a much higher power, the guy wouldn't lift a finger to help Kei, worthy mission or not.

Kei slumped his shoulders as he braced his weight on one of the gravestones. "Of all the creatures I could have gotten by mistake, it had to be you."

"Do you really expect me to believe this was an accident?"

"I don't really give a fuck what you believe, jackass. I wanted a blood demon."

"Stop calling me that."

"Then give me something else to call you." Kei snorted. "Bloody hell, it's not like I can kill you. Even weakened, you've got far too much raw power for me to challenge. Especially when I haven't come close to recovering from my offering." He raked a hand through his hair. "And why the hell would I summon an angel? I need a creature that can kill, not a holier-than-thou prick who can't so much as nick someone's skin without having a moral crisis."

The man straightened, his chest thickening as he drew himself up. Kei did his best to ignore the way the man's cock rose, heavy and hard, between his legs. The end shiny in the waning light. Damn it. Now wasn't the time to get distracted, especially by the one being he couldn't have.

"You're mistaken if you think I'm incapable of destroying you the moment I regain my power." The man smiled at Kei. "Even my soul can stand the pain of seeing the rest of your blood stain the ground."

"Great. I cast a spell for a demon and get the one angel who doesn't seem to have an issue with slaying a mage. Must be my lucky day."

"Then perhaps you shouldn't have cast the spell at all."

"I didn't summon…" Kei cursed under his breath. He'd failed. One last chance to stop a war before it destroyed a thousand worlds, and he'd somehow failed without ever getting close enough to try. He met the man's heated gaze. "If I had enough strength to send you back…" He huffed. "Guess you're stuck here until I recharge, though I'm not sure exactly how to return you, seeing as I didn't ask for your presence in the first place."

"Like you'd send me back."

"With pleasure."

The man's grim expression faltered. "Why did you summon a blood demon? You're a mage. Far more powerful than some empty shell of a beast."

"I needed something I could control—a creature that could blend in, not to mention take one hell of a beating. A way to conserve my power without abandoning my quest."

"Quest?" A harsh laugh rumbled free. "Since when is killing a quest?"

"Since it's the only way to prevent a war that won't end until every living creature in every damn realm has been purged from existence."

"War?" The man tilted his head, staring at Kei as if seeing him for the first time. "Who is it you seek?"

"Bastard's got a lot of names. You'd know him as Abaddon." Kei arched one brow. "I believe he used to be one of yours before he fell. Only, he chose his destiny."

"Abaddon? That can't be. He died when he was cast…" Disbelief shaped his features before he motioned to Kei. "Where's your army, Mage?"

"Why do you think I tried to summon a demon?"

"You're alone?" The man's mouth pinched tight, his focus shifting to the symbols still visible within the circle. "Are you mad?"

"From the moment you appeared."

The man sighed, his gaze finding Kei's again. "Gabriel."

Kei frowned. "What's that?"

"My name. It's Gabriel. And you just got far more than you bargained for."

Kei's mouth hinged open as he stared at the angel—Gabriel. Surely, the man was lying. He couldn't truly be who he claimed.

Kei drew himself up. "Gabriel? As in the archangel? All-fucking-powerful? Can kill damn near anything with a snap of his fingers...Gabriel?" He shook his head. "This isn't funny. Getting an angel is one thing. And despite the fact I sacrificed more energy than was wise, there's no way it was enough to summon a being that strong."

"Do you think I'd give you my name lightly?"

Kei backed up, his gaze sweeping the length of Gabe's body. Muscles flexed and released under his perusal, the pure beauty of his form sending a shiver down Kei's spine. He glanced away, rerunning every step he'd taken. Every word he'd uttered before he'd finished the spell, and somehow gotten...him.

Kei shook his head. "It simply can't be."

Gabe lifted his chin, a knowing smile tilting his lips. "Why would I lie about who I am, Mage?"

"The name's Kei. And I can think of a dozen different reasons as to why you'd lie to me, least of all because you're pissed." He pushed his hand through his hair, wondering what in the hell he'd done to deserve this.

Gabe's smile faded, the muscle in his temple jumping as he clenched his jaw.

Kei raised his hand in seeming defeat. "Fine. You're... Gabriel. Archangel and current pain in my ass." He crossed his arms over his chest. "So, why are you really here?"

"Are we really going to argue this again? You summoned me."

"And again, I shouldn't have gotten an angel, let alone you. The spell was fairly specific. And the last time I checked, demon and angel were pretty much opposites."

Gabe copied Kei's stance, crossing his massive arms over his chest, apparently obvious to how the simple act made his cock jut out from between his legs. He looked at the sigil carved into the ground. His brow furrowed, a hushed curse mumbling free.

Kei chuckled. "Easy, Gabe. Wouldn't want you to start sinning so soon."

Gabe glared at him, making his way over to one of the symbols on the ground. "If this is your idea of specific, you have much to learn, Ma..." He sighed. "Kei. Do you have any idea what kind of power is hidden within some of these markings?"

"Just followed the instructions, buddy. And for the record, I didn't really think I'd survive the procedure, so I didn't spend too much time worrying about what every damn symbol meant. It was supposed to grant me a worthy vessel. That's all that mattered."

Gabe shook his head. "I suggest you take better care in the future because this set of tokens has more than one translation. As for a worthy vessel..." He looked at Kei over his shoulder, tsking. "You're lucky you didn't summon Lucifer, himself, with the mix of angelic and demonic sigils you carved into the earth."

"Right, because like I said...today is definitely my lucky day."

"I'd think *not* summoning my older brother is considered extremely lucky."

Kei groaned as he walked over to Gabriel, making a point of studying the markings before shrugging. "Whatever you say. But the fact still remains... I never should have been able to summon you in the first place. Your power alone puts you in a completely different league. It doesn't make any sense." He blew out an exasperated breath. "Christ, I don't know how you even survived. But regardless, looks like you're stuck here for a while. Assuming you know the ritual to unsummon you, because that..." He waved at the circle. "Is all I could dig up on this particular spell. And it was harder than hell to decipher. I never planned on sending that demon back."

"It would appear you didn't plan on much of anything...other than dying during your ceremony."

Kei drew a shaky breath, doing his best to calm the fire licking just below the surface of his skin. If he'd known angels were this irritating, he'd have walked away and left Gabe to figure everything out for himself.

Kei motioned to the man. "You sure your brothers didn't give you the boot? Because I'd understand why they'd want to kick you out of their little club. You're annoying as hell."

Gabe straightened, his sheer presence making the air feel charged. "Only my Father or another archangel would have the strength to cast me out. I doubt it's something I'd forget."

Kei backed up a few steps. "Easy, buddy. I wasn't serious. Damn, you angels don't have much of a sense of humor, do you?" He arched a brow. "So, this is what an archangel looks like."

"What were you expecting?"

"Clothes, for one thing. Maybe more refined, less warrior worthy."

Gabe's frown intensified. "Michael isn't the only one among us who fights."

Kei chuckled. "Got some brother issues, Gabe? All I said was that you're not what I expected. Though, honestly, never thought much about angels. The one I've met isn't exactly a benchmark of greatness."

Gabe's brow furrowed as a flash of white fire gleamed in his eyes. "If what you claim is true, Abaddon isn't an angel." He turned away, adding, "At least, not anymore."

Kei felt the mixture of pain and anguish churning inside Gabriel as if the emotions were his. He rolled his shoulders against the unusual sensation, hoping it was simply a byproduct of sacrificing so much of his power. His blood. He closed the distance, nudging the other man. "I'll make you a deal."

Gabe snorted. "I don't make deals. Demons do."

Kei cursed under his breath. The jackass was infuriating at best. "It's a figure of speech. What I was going to say was...you don't second guess everything I claim, and I'll believe you in return."

Gabe drew his brows together. "I'm an angel. Why wouldn't you believe what I say?"

"Fuck. What you *are* is a piece of work. And incredibly naive. Fine. We'll discuss this later, but for now...we'd best find you some clothes and get the hell out of here before that heavenly glow of yours attracts every damn paranormal being within fifty miles. And I'm still not strong enough to start picking fights with werewolves and demons who have a hankering for angel blood."

"I don't need you to defend me, Mage."

"It's either me, or..." Kei chuckled. "Right. There isn't anyone else. Just...stick close. Full moon's not that far away, and with Samhain this close, evil is a bit stronger than usual."

Gabe huffed but fell in behind Kei as he stalked across the cemetery, the echoed cry of a wolf ringing through the surrounding trees. He could figure out their next move later—after he'd recharged. Had half a chance of surviving a confrontation. Until then, he'd babysit Gabriel. Even if the man didn't think he needed it.

ABOUT THE AUTHOR

Author, single mother, slave to chaos—she's a jack-of-all-trades who's constantly looking for her ever elusive clone.

And don't forget to subscribe to her newsletter to get the latest scoop on new and upcoming releases as well as exclusive free reads.

https://www.subscribepage.com/krisnorris

Kris loves connecting with fellow book enthusiasts. You can find her on these social media platforms...

krisnorris.ca
contactme@krisnorris.ca

f facebook.com/kris.norris.731

twitter.com/kris_norris

instagram.com/girlnovelist

a amazon.com/author/krisnorris

www.ingramcontent.com/pod-product-compliance
Lightning Source LLC
Chambersburg PA
CBHW022113170626
46808CB00002B/710